Liam needed

"About that kiss," he said, his voice heavy with the emotions pulling at him. "I'm sorry. I won't do it again."

"You said that last time."

"And I meant it last time. I'm sorry for both times."

She sighed. "So am I. We had good reasons not to do it again."

"Your life is in disarray." Though he still didn't know what that meant exactly. "How about we don't bother with the reasons, we simply agree that it's not a path forward that either of us is interested in exploring."

"That might be best," she said softly.

The aching sadness in her voice tore at his heart. "Jenna, just because I don't think we should repeat the experience, doesn't mean that wasn't an amazing kiss." He looked her directly in the eyes. "It was. Amazing, that is."

* * *

The Nanny Proposition is part of the #1 bestselling miniseries from Harlequin Desire—Billionaires and Babies: Powerful men...wrapped around their babies' little fingers.

* * *

If you're on Twitter,
tell us what you think of Harlequin Desire!
#harlequindesire

Dear Reader,

Families are great, aren't they? The best ones are full of love and support, but they sometimes come with the weight of expectations. It might be that you're the oldest child, so you have to be "the responsible one" and look after younger siblings, or it might be assuming that you'll make the family proud. My grandmother's sister was expected to stay home and look after her parents instead of having a job or marrying—potential suitors were driven off!

So what happens if you don't live up to the expectations?

In *The Nanny Proposition,* I wanted to look at two people who've grown up with pretty heavy family expectations. Two people who are each single parents to a baby and need each other on a whole range of levels.

Princess Jensine Larson has lived with family expectations her entire life...until she stumbled by getting pregnant out of wedlock. Liam Hawke has never questioned that he would work in the family business and be a success like his parents and brothers, but his baby's maternal family expect him to fail as a father, which is one expectation he's determined *not* to meet.

This is the first book about the Hawke brothers, but Dylan and Adam's stories are on their way.

I hope you enjoy Liam and Jenna's (and Bonnie's and Meg's!) story.

Cheers,

Rachel

THE NANNY PROPOSITION

RACHEL BAILEY

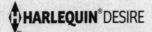

Recycling programs
for this product may
not exist in your area.

ISBN-13: 978-0-373-73332-3

THE NANNY PROPOSITION

Printed in U.S.A.

RACHEL BAILEY

developed a serious book addiction at a young age (via Peter Rabbit and Jemima Puddle-Duck) and has never recovered. Just how she likes it. She went on to earn degrees in psychology and social work, but is now living her dream—writing romance for a living.

She lives on a piece of paradise on Australia's Sunshine Coast with her hero and four dogs, where she loves to sit with a dog or two, overlooking the trees and reading books from her evergrowing to-be-read pile.

Rachel would love to hear from you and can be contacted through her website, www.rachelbailey.com.

This book is for all the writing dogs who've kept me company. Not every dog I've had has been a writing dog, but a few have made it part of their role: Sascha, my first writing dog, who lay in her basket beside my desk and kept my writing time safe by growling at anyone—human or dog—who entered the room. Oliver, who sleeps nearby when I write and reminds me to keep my chocolate levels up (and to toss him a dog chocolate while I'm at it). Fergus, who likes to sleep under my desk, dreaming his dog dreams. Dougal, who ensures I don't spend too long at my desk in each stint by nudging me to take him for a game of dog tennis. Roxie, who sits on the lounge beside me during writing days at my mother's house. And especially Jazzie May, who passed away while I was writing *The Nanny Proposition*. In between perimeter patrols and naps by the office door, she'd sit by my desk and give me her big smile and ask if I needed anything—a dog to pat, perhaps? Hugs to you, my Jasmine Maybelline.

Acknowledgments

Thanks to my editor, Charles Griemsman, who has a fabulous eye for story and the patience of a saint. Also to Amanda Ashby for the brainstorming and waffles, and Claire Baxter, who helped create a new country. And Cheryl Lemon for the information on California (though any mistakes are mine). But mostly, thanks to Barbara DeLeo and Sharon Archer, the best critique partners in the world.

One

Liam Hawke held the cell phone tightly against his ear, but it didn't help. The person on the other end of the phone wasn't making any sense.

"Mr. Hawke? Are you there?"

"Hang on a moment," he said and pulled his Jeep to the side of the road. At his brother's enquiring stare, Liam said in an undertone, "Listen," and hit the speaker button on his cell. "Can you repeat that, please?"

"I'm a midwife at the Sacred Heart Hospital and I just informed you that you've become a father. Congratulations." Liam frowned, Dylan's eyes widened and the woman continued. "Your daughter, Bonnie, is two days old and still here with her mother. Unfortunately, her mother has had some complications following the birth and has asked me to contact you. It would be best if you came right away."

A baby? Dylan mouthed as Liam loosened his tie

and undid the top button on his shirt, which had suddenly become too tight. There had to be a mistake. Babies didn't magically appear. Usually there was nine months' notice, for one thing.

The L.A. sun shone down on them through the sunroof as Liam swallowed and tried to get his voice to work. "Are you sure you have the right person?"

"You're Liam John Hawke?" she asked.

"I am."

"You were in a relationship with Rebecca Clancy?"

"Yes" —if you could call their arrangement a relationship— "but she wasn't pregnant when we broke up." Which had been a good while ago. He struggled to remember when he'd last seen her but couldn't bring a time or place to mind.

How long *had* it been? It could have been eight months ago.... An uncomfortable heat crawled across his skin. Then another piece of information registered. "You said Rebecca had some complications. Is she all right?"

The midwife drew in a measured breath. "I think it would be better if we spoke in person."

"I'll be there as soon as I can," he said and disconnected. He pulled the Jeep back out into the flow of traffic and made a U-turn.

Dylan pulled out his cell. "I'll cancel the meeting."

When Dylan ended the call, Liam threw him a tight smile. "Thanks."

"You had no idea?" Dylan asked.

"I still have no idea." He ran a hand through his hair, then brought it back to grip the wheel. "Sure, I was dating Rebecca back then, but that doesn't prove I'm the father of her baby." He'd heard she'd been dating again soon after their breakup. First order of business would be a paternity test.

After a frustrating delay in L.A. traffic, they arrived at the hospital. They made their way to the neonatal unit, where they were greeted by a woman in a pale blue uniform. She led them through to the nursery. "Ms. Clancy took a turn for the worse after I called you, and she's been taken back to surgery. Her parents went up with her, so they've left Bonnie with us here in the nursery." She leaned over and picked up a bundle of soft pink blanket with a tiny face peeping out.

"Hello, sweetheart," she cooed. "Your daddy's here to meet you."

Before Liam could head the nurse off with an explanation about needing a paternity test, she'd placed the baby in his arms. Large eyes fringed by long dark lashes blinked open and looked up at him. Her tiny pale pink face seemed so fragile, yet somehow more real than anything else in the room.

"I'll leave you two to get to know each other for a few minutes," the midwife said. "There's a comfy chair over there in the corner."

Dylan cleared his throat. "I'll just…ah…pop out and get us a couple of coffees."

But Liam was only vaguely paying attention to them. Bonnie was all he could see. He couldn't remember the last time he'd held a baby and he wasn't one-hundred-percent sure he was doing it right, but he held her closer and breathed in her clean, sweet smell. He could feel the warmth of her body through the blanket, and a ghost of a smile crept across his face.

All three Hawke brothers had their mother's unusual hair color of darkest brown shot through with deep red—and Bonnie already had a thick crop of hair exactly that shade. He'd still demand a paternity test, no question, and he'd need to have a full and frank discussion with Rebecca, but he was sure of one thing: Bonnie was his.

She was a Hawke.

As he sank into the chair and stared into the eyes of his daughter, the world stilled. *His baby.* His heart clenched tight, then expanded to fill his chest, his body. And for the first time in his life, Liam Hawke fell head over heels in love.

He lost track of time as he sat there, holding his daughter and telling her stories about her new family, of her two uncles and of his parents, who would adore and spoil their first grandchild rotten. An hour ago he was on his way to a business meeting with Dylan for their family company, Hawke's Blooms. How had his day gone from thinking about the business of growing and selling flowers to thinking about a having a little girl in his life?

A movement out of the corner of his eye made him look up to see a middle-aged couple enter the nursery. They stumbled to a halt just inside the door. "Who are you?" the heavily made-up woman demanded.

Instinctively, he held Bonnie a little tighter. This had to be Rebecca's parents. He'd never met them when he'd dated Rebecca—given the relationship had barely lasted three months before he'd ended it, the opportunity had never arisen. He guessed he'd be seeing more of them now.

"Liam Hawke," he said calmly, politely. "Bonnie's father."

Scowling, the man stepped forward on one Italian-shoed foot. "How do you even know about Bonnie?"

"Rebecca asked the nurse to call me." Not wanting

to disrupt the baby, he stayed in the chair and kept his voice level. "But the real question is, why *wouldn't* I know about her?"

"Rebecca would never have done that," the woman said, her eyes narrowing. "When Rebecca's discharged, she and the baby will be coming back to live with us—she moved in two months ago. We'll raise Bonnie together. In fact, you can hand her over now and leave before Rebecca gets out of surgery. If she'd wanted to see you, she'd have mentioned it before now."

Liam took a breath, prepared to give the couple some slack given their daughter was in surgery. But they were seriously mistaken if they thought he was going anywhere.

"So your plan was to never tell me I have a child?" he asked and met their gazes steadily.

"Rebecca's plan," the man corrected.

Their arrogance was astounding. To deliberately keep a baby's birth—the existence of a person—secret was beyond comprehension. "She didn't think I'd want to know? That Bonnie would need a father?"

The woman sniffed. "You can't provide anything that she won't already have. Your wealth is nothing to ours. And she'll have people around her *capable* of love."

He heard the unspoken critique of his family's wealth clear enough—the Hawke family didn't just have less money, they had *new* money. He felt his blood pressure rise another notch. He'd come across the prejudice often, always from people who'd never put in a hard day's work in their lives, whose riches had been passed down and all they'd had to do was spend and perhaps adjust the investments. He'd never been able to conjure up any respect for someone who'd inherited their money and position.

About to respond, Liam frowned and paused. Something in that last dig had been especially pointed. What exactly had Rebecca told them about him? They hadn't broken up on the best of terms, sure, but he hadn't thought it had been too bad. Though, now that he thought about it, hadn't Rebecca talked about her parents being cold and manipulative? Was this coming from Rebecca or from them…?

A man in a surgeon's gown appeared in the doorway. His face was drawn as he took off the paper cap that had covered his hair. "Mr. and Mrs. Clancy?"

"Yes?" Rebecca's mother grabbed her husband's hand. "Is she out of surgery? How is she?"

"I'm afraid I have some bad news. Rebecca fought hard, but her body had—"

"She's gone?" Mr. Clancy said, his voice hoarse.

The doctor nodded. "I'm sorry."

Mrs. Clancy let out a loud, broken sob and slumped against her husband, who pulled her against him. The noise made Bonnie's face crumple, then she began to wail. Stunned, Liam looked down at her. Her mother had just died. She was motherless. Her life would always be affected by this one tragic incident.

And he had no idea what to do.

The midwife rushed through the door, jostling to get past the doctor, who was still talking to Rebecca's parents, and took Bonnie from him. Liam watched her soothe Bonnie as if from a distance. As if it wasn't really happening.

"I'm so sorry about the news, Mr. Hawke," she said.

"What—" He cleared his throat. "What happens to Bonnie now?"

"Rebecca had already filled in the birth certificate and named you as the father. So as far as the hospital is concerned, you have custody of her. If you don't want her, I know Rebecca's parents were talking about raising her. How about I call the social worker to help you sort through your options?"

Bonnie had calmed down to a mild hiccup. Bonnie. His baby. She had worked her little arm free from the blanket and was waving it in the air. He reached out to touch her tiny fist, enclosing it in his.

"There's no need," he said and met the midwife's gaze. "Bonnie will live with me. I'll raise my own daughter."

The midwife smiled in approval. "We'll show you some basics, like how to feed her, then you'll be on your way. She's already had all her tests and passed everything with flying colors."

Liam blinked. Now? Just like that? He knew next to nothing about babies....

Suddenly Rebecca's mother was in front of them, making a grab for the baby. "I'll take her," she said, shooting Liam a defiant look. "We're going home."

Unperturbed, the midwife handed Bonnie to Liam. "I'm sorry, but Mr. Hawke is her father. Your daughter named him on the birth certificate. He has custody."

Mr. Clancy came to stand beside his wife and narrowed reddened eyes at Liam. "We'll see about that. He's not fit to raise a baby and I'll say that in court if I have to."

Liam didn't flinch. The Clancys could try whatever they liked. No one was taking his daughter from him.

As Jenna arranged the last of the weekly flower delivery—fragrant jasmine and sunshine-yellow lilies today—into a crystal vase, she heard her boss, Dylan Hawke, arrive home from an all-nighter. Judging by the voices coming from the penthouse foyer, his brother Liam was with him. Liam had a smooth, deep voice that always made her melt....

And that *is a completely inappropriate way to think about your employer's family.* Or any man. It had been falling for a man and forgetting her duty that had put her in this position.

She gathered up the flower stems she'd trimmed and ducked into the hall before the men made it into the living room. One of the things she'd learned growing up in a royal palace was that housekeepers were expected to keep a low profile—like magic cleaning and cooking fairies who were rarely seen.

From the adjoining kitchen, she heard a baby's cry and she stilled. It sounded like the cry of a newborn. Her arms ached for her own little Meg, but she was in day care, and at eight months old, her cry was different. Her boss, Dylan, and his two brothers, Liam and Adam, were all bachelors, and none of Dylan's friends had been expecting as far as she knew. She'd been pregnant herself for part of the time she'd worked here, so an expectant mother would have caught her attention.

Footsteps sounded down the hall, and then Dylan's face appeared around the corner. "Jenna, we could use your help with a slight baby problem."

"Sure," she said, wiping her hands and following him back out. The Santa Monica penthouse apartment's large living room was decorated in whites and neutrals so the only spots of color were the flowers she'd just arranged and the two men who stood in the center, one awkwardly holding the tiny bundle that was now crying loudly. Jenna breathed an "ohhh," her arms aching with the need to comfort the little thing.

As they approached, Liam glanced up at his brother,

then back to the baby he was gently jiggling. Even as her heart sighed at the sight of the six-foot-plus man with the tiny pink bundle, Jenna frowned. Who would leave their new baby with two clueless men? Despite being respected and feared businessmen, they were clearly out of their depth.

"Liam," Dylan said. "You remember Jenna. She'll know what to do."

Jenna glanced at her boss and asked in an undertone, "What to do about what, exactly?"

He stared blankly at her and then shrugged. "About the baby," he whispered.

Right. Well, maybe if she could calm the baby, she could find out what she needed to do.

"Yes," she said, her eyes on the little person nestled in Liam's strong arms. "Maybe I can help?"

Liam regarded her with an assessing gaze—he was less certain of her ability. He needed help—that was evident from the baby's cries becoming more desperate and the awkward way he was holding her—but his eyes held a fierce protectiveness. He wasn't handing this baby over to just anyone. She respected that—in fact, the sight of a man being so protective brought a lump of emotion to her throat. She'd have to lay his fears to rest if she was going to help.

"Hi, Mr. Hawke," she said, smiling brightly. "I'm not sure you remember me, but I'm Jenna Peters." She generally tried to stay out of the way when Dylan had guests, so she and Liam had never had a conversation, but she hoped he might at least recognize her.

He nodded in acknowledgment, but he then turned his attention back to the tiny, squirming girl he held.

"I have an eight-month-old daughter, Meg, and she cried like this when I first brought her home. Would you like me to try some of the tricks I learned with Meg on this little girl?"

Liam looked down at the baby, stroked a fingertip softly down her cheek, took a deep breath and oh-so-carefully placed the baby in Jenna's arms.

"Bonnie," he said, his voice rough. "Her name is Bonnie."

As he said the name, his dark green eyes softened and Jenna's stomach looped. He was still standing close, as if not wanting to be too far from the baby. Jenna shivered. She could feel the heat from his body, see the day's growth of dark beard, smell the masculine scent of his skin....

She stepped back, away from this man's aura. The priority here was Bonnie.

Jenna pulled the pale pink blanket a bit more firmly around the little girl, laid her across her heart so the baby could feel the beat and began to pace and rock, crooning as she went. The cries gradually quieted until a wet-faced Bonnie peered up at her.

"Hello, little one," Jenna murmured, unable to stop the smile spreading across her face.

Dylan crept across to look over Jenna's shoulder. "Good work, Jenna," he whispered.

But Jenna's gaze was drawn to Liam. He looked from the baby across to her, his features holding too many emotions to be easily deciphered, though gratitude was definitely one of them. He and this baby must have a strong link—perhaps they were related, or he was close to the parents.

He cleared his throat. "How did you do that?"

"I've laid her over my heart," she said, smoothing the fine, dark hair on Bonnie's head. "Babies like to feel the beat."

"Thank you," he said. His voice was low and full of sincerity.

She glanced up and opened her mouth to tell him he was welcome, but her throat suddenly refused to cooperate. She'd been around Dylan's brothers before, enough to know that good looks and hair like dark, polished mahogany ran in the family, but she'd never before been exposed to the full force of Liam Hawke's intensity. He looked like Dylan, yet nothing like him. Liam's hair gleamed in the sunlight streaming through the tall windows. His eyes didn't sparkle like her boss's; they simmered, a deep green maelstrom focused on her.

She swallowed and forced her mouth to work. "She's lovely. Are you looking after her?"

"You could say that," he said, his voice flat. "Her mother died."

Her heart breaking for the little girl, Jenna stared down at the baby who was drifting off to sleep. "Oh, I'm so sorry. Is she yours?"

"Yes," Liam said. A world of meaning was in that one word.

She lifted a hand to touch his forearm but thought better of it and laid it back around Bonnie. This man was still her boss's brother.

Dylan moved closer and looked over Jenna's shoulder. "Before we left the hospital, they showed Liam how to look after her. And while he was doing that, I ducked out and got a baby seat fitted to his Jeep. But once we hit the road, she started crying and nothing we did seemed to help. I suggested that when he dropped me off, he come up and see if you could get Bonnie settled before he drove home."

She sneaked a glance at Liam, curious about the circumstances that had led to this situation. Curious about why he didn't already have a car seat fitted when he went to pick up a baby. Curious about him. Instead she asked, "Could she be hungry?"

Liam shook his head. "She shouldn't be. We fed her last thing before we left the hospital."

"She's settled now," Jenna said. "Would you like to take her back?"

He nodded, but she saw the uncertainty in his eyes. Jenna positioned the baby across his chest, unable to avoid touching his shirt, then stepped back.

Bonnie squirmed, then settled as her father stroked her back.

"You live alone downstairs, don't you?" Liam asked, his gaze not leaving his daughter.

"On the bottom floor with my little girl." Dylan's apartment had three floors—Dylan slept on the top and she and Meg were on the lowest level. Luckily noise didn't travel in this apartment so Meg didn't disturb Dylan.

Jenna had been working as his housekeeper for more than a year now. She'd applied for the job at four-months' pregnant, and he'd been good to her, more than she'd expected from an employer. Having a job that gave her a place to live as well as an income was exactly what she'd needed in her situation.

An unmarried princess from the ancient royal family of Larsland falling pregnant had been intolerable, so Princess Jensine Larsen had left her homeland before anyone found out and started a new life in Los Angeles as Jenna Peters. But she had no support network, no family, no friends to fall back on. This job with Dylan had been a godsend and she didn't want to jeopardize it.

"I really need to get back—" she said as she turned away, but Liam cut her off.

"Where's your baby while you work?"

Jenna thought about the most precious thing in her life and held back a wince. "She's in day care."

"Wouldn't you prefer to have her with you?"

Jenna hesitated, looking from Liam to Dylan and back to Liam. The answer was obvious, but her boss was sitting in the room. "In an ideal world, of course I'd like to spend all day with my daughter." Even if she were at home giving Meg a royal upbringing, they wouldn't see much of each other—Meg would be raised by nannies and nursery staff, as Jenna herself had been. "But I need to earn a living to support us both, and I'm prepared to make sacrifices for that. Dylan's been good to me. I'm really grateful for this job. Speaking of which," she said, edging out of the room, "I have to go—"

"Wait," he said, and despite herself, she stopped.

Liam looked into the clear blue eyes of his brother's housekeeper. "I'm going to need help with Bonnie."

She nodded and smiled encouragingly. "That's probably a good idea," she said in her musical Scandinavian accent. "Being a single parent is a hard road. Will your parents help?"

That would have been best, and if he'd known he was about to become a father, he could probably have arranged it. He rubbed his fingertips across his forehead. "My parents are overseas for a couple of months."

Dylan let out an ironic chuckle. "They'd been looking forward to their big European holiday, but it turns out it was bad timing."

"You might want to think about hiring a nanny," Jenna said.

That had been his thought exactly. When the midwife had handed the tiny bundle to him, Liam had awkwardly accepted Bonnie and held her against his chest. He'd played a lot of sports in his life and coaches had often told him he had natural grace and agility. Yet he wasn't comfortable holding his own daughter. At least his heart knew no such awkwardness—in that moment, with his baby clasped to him, his heart had expanded as if it could reach out and encompass both of them with a love stronger than anything he'd ever experienced.

When they'd arrived at Dylan's penthouse, he'd held a fussy, sad-eyed Bonnie, and the sight had slayed him. He'd move heaven and Earth for this little girl, but she hadn't seemed to want anything from him. Now, if everything went to plan, he'd found somebody she would want—Jenna Peters.

And he was going to get her for Bonnie.

Liam looked at his younger brother. "You're going to do me a favor, Dylan."

"I am?" he said, folding his arms across his chest. "What is it?"

"You're going to let your housekeeper go without serving out her notice."

Dylan slowly uncrossed his arms and planted his hands low on his hips. "Why would I do that? I like Jenna."

Liam smiled, feeling the satisfaction of a good plan coming together. "She can't be your housekeeper because she's about to become my nanny."

"Your nanny?" Jenna said, her pale eyebrows drawing together. "I'm not leaving my job."

"Not just a nanny. You'll also teach me how to be a parent."

"You're already her father."

"I might be her father, but parenting is not part of my skill set." He shifted his weight to his other leg. Admitting a weakness so freely was tough, but he had to be completely honest if he wanted this to work. "I need to learn how to take care of a baby and bond with her. Circumstances mean I haven't had time to prepare for this and I'm not willing for Bonnie to suffer while I'm catching up. You'd be something of a parenthood coach."

Bonnie's grandparents had been furious that he'd been sent home with her, but he'd left them to their grief over losing Rebecca. He expected to hear from them soon about a bid for custody, and he'd deal with that when it happened. For now, he was focused on the immediate future. On being exactly what Bonnie needed.

"I'm no expert," Jenna said, shaking her head. "Many other people are more qualified for that. Agencies devoted to nannies and babysitters."

He glanced pointedly at his daughter, now sleeping soundly, then back to Jenna. "Bonnie seems to disagree."

"Getting a tired baby to sleep is one thing. I'm still working out so many other things as I go along through trial and error. Of course, I read books and articles." She tucked a strand of blond hair that had escaped her ponytail behind her ear, somehow making the simple gesture elegant. "But sometimes I'm just guessing."

He shrugged. None of that worried him—he'd already assumed as much. "You're many steps ahead of me. You'll share what you know and I'll pick it up as we go along. It won't take long before I'll know everything I need to know about babies."

Her eyebrows lifted to almost her hairline and she seemed uncertain about whether to laugh or not. She didn't believe him. That was fine—she didn't know him. He'd never shied from a challenge before, and this challenge was about his daughter. He wouldn't fail.

"So, you'll take the job?"

"Thing is, this is more than a job—it's my home too." She tapped her fingers against her lips, drawing his attention to their softly curved shape. "What will happen to me once you know all you need to know? I have a stable job and home for my daughter here, and I'm sure Dylan would replace me fairly quickly so I wouldn't be able to come back."

"Even when you've finished coaching me in the role of parent, I'll still need a nanny, at least until she goes to school. You won't be kicked out on the street."

She chewed on her lip, and he could see her mind going at a hundred miles an hour, thinking through all the possibilities. He liked that trait in his daughter's nanny. Hell, he liked that trait in anyone.

Jenna rubbed a delicate finger across her forehead. "Can I think about it?"

"I'd prefer you didn't. As you can see, I'm on my way home now. I only stopped in here to drop Dylan off and I wanted to try and settle her before the drive out of town. I'd like you to come with me and help with the feeding and bathing from the start."

"Now?" she asked, blue eyes widening.

"Pack a bag and we'll pick up Meg on the way. I'll send a moving company over to grab the rest of your things tomorrow."

"Hey, what about me?" Dylan asked, looking at them in bewilderment.

Liam waved the concern away with a flick of his wrist. "I'm sure you'll survive without a housekeeper until you can get an agency to send over a temp." He turned back to Jenna. "You'll take it?"

She lifted a hand to circle her throat, looking from him to Dylan and back again. "But—"

"Don't overanalyze it, Jenna. I have a job vacancy and you're qualified to fill it. I'll match the wage Dylan is paying you with a twenty percent raise, and the job comes with accommodation. Best of all, you can keep your baby with you during the day instead of having her in day care. Just say yes. Go on—" he smiled "—you know you want to. Say yes."

Her eyes flicked back to his brother. "Go on," Dylan said, clearly resigned to being housekeeper-less in the short term. "If you want the job, take it. I'll be fine. My brother and my niece need you more than I do right now."

"Yes," she said, then bit down on her lip, as if surprised at herself. Then more firmly, "Yes."

"Excellent." Liam stood, ready to leave now the solution could be put into place. "How long will you take to pack a bag?"

"If you give me your address, I can throw a few things together and catch a cab over in about an hour."

"I'll wait." He wanted her there when he and Bonnie arrived home. He was pretty sure Bonnie would need changing or feeding or both. "You and Meg can come with me and the movers can do everything else."

"Now," she said, a touch of wonder in her voice. "Okay, I'll go and pack a couple of bags as quickly as I can."

Liam let out a long breath as he watched his new nanny head down the hallway. There was something beautiful in the way she moved—he could watch her just walk all day. Having her under the same roof would be no hardship.

Before he could let that thought take hold, he gave himself a mental shake. He had bigger issues than attraction to a beautiful woman. In fact, attraction would be downright problematic. Now that he'd solved the problem of what to do with Bonnie, he wouldn't jeopardize that solution by acting like a teenager ruled by his hormones. He knew how to behave himself, knew what needed to be off-limits. Nothing would jeopardize this plan.

Everything was going to be all right.

He glanced down at Bonnie, sleeping in his arms. No, everything would be better than all right. He'd make sure of it.

Two

The trip in Liam's Jeep to his home in San Juan Capistrano was awkwardly silent after Meg's babble as she played with a crinkly toy in the back subsided and she eventually dozed off. By the time Jenna had finished packing a couple of bags of her and Meg's things, Bonnie had been hungry so they'd fed her before setting off. Now the baby was asleep too.

Behind the shield of her sunglasses, Jenna sneaked a look at her new employer. He sat tall in the driver's seat—she knew he had an inch or two on Dylan's six feet—and faint frown lines streaked across his forehead. Those lines were absent from his brother's face. But minor differences to his brothers didn't come close to explaining why it was *this* brother who'd always caught her eye. Why on those rare occasions his gaze had fallen on her at Dylan's apartment over the year, her heart had beaten that little bit faster.

What did she really know about him—well, besides that he was a man used to getting his own way? She'd been swept along by the speed with which he'd acted. She was used to autocratic people—not only was her mother a ruling monarch, but her father and siblings were all princes and princesses who were used to having people, including her, obey them.

She'd needed that job with Dylan, the settledness of it, the security of it for her and her daughter, yet here she was after only a matter of hours, minutes really, being relocated to Liam's house. Why had she let that happen?

As hard to resist as he was, she knew it was Bonnie's plight that called to her. And Liam's reaction to his new daughter—he was bumbling with his inexperience but so very protective and determined to do the best by the baby.

Most people had nine months to get used to the idea of parenthood. While she'd fed Bonnie at Dylan's apartment, Liam had admitted he'd had less than twenty-four hours since being thrust into the role of instant father.

And it was her job to help him acclimatize. Time to step into her role.

"I'm assuming you don't have any baby supplies at home?" she said, breaking the silence.

"Supplies?" He shoved one hand through his hair, then gripped the wheel again. "I have the car seat Dylan had fitted and the hospital gave me some things."

"Oh, well that will do for a start, but you'll need much more than that."

"I will?" he asked, his dark brows drawing together above aviator sunglasses.

"Yes." She fished around in her handbag, found a pen and scrap of paper and started making notes. They'd need everything from bedding to clothing to kitchen supplies.... "She'll need a few pieces of furniture besides a crib. A chest of drawers or a cupboard for her clothes, and maybe a chair we can put in her room for night feeds. But we can use whatever you have."

"I'll show you around and you can take what you need from other rooms." His voice was deep and business-like, as if he was organizing the logistics for a project. "Put everything else on your list and I'll get a baby shop to deliver."

"We don't need all of this right away," she said, looking down at the crumpled bit of paper in her hand. It was going to be a big delivery to get everything at once—she'd bought Meg's things slowly, in batches. "With some things, we can make do or she can use Meg's."

"Don't be shy about ordering new things for her. If Bonnie needs it, she gets it."

"Okay. We're going to need formula, diapers, bottles, a sterilizer, a crib, crib sheets, blankets, a diaper bag—"

Liam held up a hand. "What's a diaper bag? Don't they arrive in a bag?"

"It's to put all her baby supplies in when we take her out. Actually," she said, making a note, "we'd better get two." She scanned to find her place in the list. "Monitor, high chair, baby wash, booties, onesies—"

Liam stopped her again. "All of this for one seven-pound baby?" he asked incredulously. "Seriously?"

She held back a smile. "Amazing, isn't it? And this is just to start."

She kept reading, and though his eyes were hidden behind his dark sunglasses and he didn't interrupt her again, she sensed his air of bemusement.

When they pulled up in front of the house, Jenna was surprised. She'd expected something sleek and modern, like Dylan's penthouse, but this was older and rambling. Two stories high, tall windows with sashed curtains, wide verandas of varnished wood and the air of a family home.

Liam parked in front of the main door, under a portico, and jumped out.

They unbuckled the babies and Jenna followed Liam into the house, she carrying an instantly awake and perky Meg, and Liam carrying a still-sleeping Bonnie in one strong arm.

The house was spacious and open plan, with living areas connected by archways. The whole was decorated in neutrals with splashes of color, like the burnt orange rugs on the tiled floor and olive green cushions on the sofa. It was sophisticated but much more relaxed than Dylan's apartment. More of a home. Jenna smiled. Bonnie would love growing up here.

A woman appeared through one of the archways, tall, silent and grim-faced.

Liam glanced up and nodded at the woman. "There you are, Katherine."

"Do you need something, Mr. Hawke?" she asked, moving very few facial muscles in the action.

"Just to introduce you to our newcomers." He held an encompassing arm out in their direction. "Jenna, this is Katherine, my housekeeper. Katherine, this is Jenna and her baby, Meg. As I mentioned on the phone, Jenna is going to be Bonnie's nanny. I'm not really sure how these things work. I understand babies create a lot of washing and mess, so you'll need to work together. Perhaps you also can take on a part-timer to help with the extra workload."

Katherine didn't spare Jenna a glance. "I told you I could take care of the little one, Mr. Hawke."

Liam didn't seem fazed. "You already have a full-time job, Katherine. You're essential to this household, and I won't have you overburdened."

Katherine sniffed, appearing to be partially mollified. "I assume there will be one extra for dinner?"

Liam nodded. "And for all meals now, thank you."

"I'll be in the kitchen if you need me." Still without acknowledging Jenna, Katherine turned and left.

Jenna watched the other woman leave. She hadn't been so thoroughly snubbed since she was twelve and her sister Eva had told her she was too babyish to come to her fourteenth birthday party.

"Did I do something wrong?" she asked.

"That's just Katherine," he said and shrugged casually. "She's run this place like a captain runs a ship for eight years and I'd be lost without her, but she can be a little…territorial."

Territorial was one word. Rude was another. "But you said she couldn't do both jobs anyway."

"Knowing Katherine," he said with the hint of a smile, "she would have liked to have made that decision for herself, then been the one who hired the new nanny."

Oh, good. That promised to play out well. Jenna took a breath and changed the subject. "Have you lived here long?"

"Since I was eleven. My parents bought it as a little farmhouse, not much more than a shack really, but it was the land they wanted. As the business grew, we added rooms." He looked around at the house as if it were an old friend. "I bought it from my parents five years ago when they wanted to retire and move off the farm. It is a good arrangement—they moved to a nice apartment in the city with no maintenance, and I can live here next to my work."

She followed his gaze, taking in all the tasteful elegance that oozed money. "It's hard to imagine this place as a shack."

"The original structure is now storerooms off the laundry. But for now, I'll show you the bedrooms I thought we could use as the nurseries."

"You're thinking of giving them their own nursery each?"

He put the keys to the Jeep and his sunglasses on a hall stand, then readjusted Bonnie to hold her closer before turning back to face Jenna. "If we don't, Bonnie will wake Meg when it's time for her night feeds and we'll end up having to get two babies back to sleep."

"It would be great if they could have their own rooms—I just wasn't sure how much space you had. I thought Meg might sleep in with me."

"Up here," he said as he walked up a staircase, "is the main bedroom wing. My bedroom is this one at the end." He opened a door and she peeked in to see a huge room decorated in strong browns and cream with a forest green wall behind the bed. Being at the end of the wing, it had windows on three sides that showcased amazing panoramic views of the San Juan Capistrano countryside.

He strode back down the hallway to the first room and ushered her in. "This is one of the guest bedrooms. There are three along this hall. I was thinking you could have this one. Then the next room for Meg, and the one beside mine for Bonnie."

The rooms were sumptuously decorated, each in a different color. The room that was to be hers had been done in lavender and wheat, with a satin comforter on the four-poster bed and a series of beautifully framed close-up shots of purple irises on the wall. It was gorgeous but didn't seem either Liam's or Katherine's style.

She stepped in and ran a hand over the silky bed cover. "Did you choose this color scheme?"

"No, my mother had the house redecorated before she and my father moved out a few years ago."

She walked into the next room along and turned around. Meg's new nursery had mint green walls and accents in rose pink. The bed had a multihued knitted blanket, and on the walls was a photo series of bright pink tulips. "We should easily fit Meg's crib and changing table in here along with the bed."

"No problem to move the bed out if you want."

Her eyes were drawn back to the bedcover. "Who knitted the blanket?"

"My mother," he said, a trace of a smile flitting across his face. "My brothers and I each have several of them."

"And the flower photos?" she asked, pointing to the tulips.

"They're mine. I take lots of photos in the greenhouse for records. My mother had some of them framed."

His tone was dismissive, but these were more than mere record keeping. The way the light had been captured hitting the leaves and the angle chosen to accentuate the shape of the petals were masterful. However, she didn't think he'd appreciate her pointing that out, so she let it drop.

The room next to his, Bonnie's nursery, had the same tasteful and elegant feel, but it was full of dark wood and tan walls. Masculine and heavy. Perfect for a male guest, but not so appropriate for a baby girl's room.

Liam winced and threw her an apologetic glance. "Perhaps you could organize this room to be painted."

"Absolutely. Any thoughts on color?"

"I'll leave that to you," he said, glancing out the window and seemingly distracted. "I'll organize a credit card—it will make redecorating this room and obtaining ongoing things for Bonnie easier. Though if it's something regular, like formula or diapers, let Katherine know and she can add it to the grocery order."

"Okay."

Bonnie fussed in his arms, and Liam's eyes suddenly had an edge of panic.

Jenna put Meg on the floor with a rattle from her handbag. "Do you want me to take her?"

"That might be best," he said and gently handed her over.

Jenna looked down at the sweet little baby and ran her hand over the soft, downy hair. "Her hair is so dark. Like yours, actually. Meg was bald when she was born."

A smile flittered across his mouth then left. "Bonnie's hair was how I knew for sure she was mine at the hospital." Frowning, he threw a glance to the door. "Listen, I know you've just arrived, but I need to duck out to the greenhouse. I hadn't expected to miss work this morning, so there are things I need to check on."

"No problem," she said, taking the cue. "You go back to work. We'll be fine here."

It seemed it had only been a couple of hours since she'd given Liam the list when a small truck with a stork emblazoned on the side pulled into the paved circular driveway. Liam had obviously found a place that was willing to deliver immediately. It probably helped that money talked.

Two young men jumped out and, with Meg on her hip, she met them at the front door. Bonnie was asleep in Liam's room in an old basinet Katherine had found. Since Liam's room was the farthest away from the rest of the house, she'd put the baby down there for the nap, hoping to not disturb her while they set up the nurseries. "We have a delivery for Liam Hawke," the older man said.

"You've got the right place. Thanks for being so quick."

"All part of the service," he said. They walked to the truck, rolled up the back and started to unload. Jenna showed them the way to Bonnie's nursery. The men assembled the new furniture in the living room and left piles of pastel pink crib sheets, blankets and other supplies stacked on the dining room table. Bonnie was lucky that her every need would be taken care of, that she wouldn't want for anything—yet, there was something a little sad about all her personal things being delivered like a work order. Nothing had been handpicked by someone who loved her.

Though…*had* things already been bought for her? Bonnie's mother must have been prepared for a newborn. Had she lovingly chosen little clothes, searched for and selected a charming crib and linen? Dreamed about playing lullabies as her baby went to sleep? Jenna's throat felt thick with emotion.

"That's it," the delivery man said from behind her. "Mr. Hawke paid over the phone, so I just need you to sign for the delivery." He handed her a clipboard with some papers attached.

"Thanks," she said, taking the clipboard then setting Meg down on the carpet.

As she put pen to paper to sign for the order, she hesitated for a moment before remembering her name. Jenna Peters. She'd had the name for more than a year now; surely soon it would become second nature to use it?

But even as she signed the fake name and handed the

form back, she knew the truth—she'd always be Princess Jensine Larsen, youngest of the five children of the reigning queen of Larsland. A princess who'd never put a foot wrong in her twenty-three years until she made one mistake big enough to obliterate that record.

She'd become pregnant out of wedlock.

At first the news hadn't been too bad—she and Alexander were in love and had been planning to marry one day. They'd just have to move the date forward. And tell their families. Their relationship had been a secret—after a life lived in the public eye, she'd just wanted one thing that was hers alone. She grimaced. People always said to be careful what you wish for. Now her entire life was lived in secret.

They'd planned on telling their families when Alexander came home from his latest military deployment. But Alexander hadn't come home. He'd been killed in the line of duty, leaving her grieving and pregnant, with no chance of salvaging her honor.

She hadn't been able to tell her parents and face their disappointment. Perhaps worst of all, once the local press found out, it would have tarnished the reputation of the royal family, something she'd been brought up to avoid at all costs. A royal family that had, unlike many of its European neighbors, avoided any hint of scandal in its modern history. The situation would have dealt Larsland royalty its final blow in an age when people were questioning the need for royalty at all.

She'd only been able to see one way out. She'd fled the country and set up a new identity in Los Angeles with the aid of a childhood friend, Kristen, who now worked in the royal security patrol. Jenna had originally planned to run to the United Kingdom because she'd been there before and it had a population large enough to lose herself in, but Kristen had a friend in the United States who'd worked with her on an exchange program a couple of years ago and was now in a position to help. Kristen and her U.S. counterpart were now the only two people who knew both who she really was and precisely where she was. She was sure her parents would have used her passport's trail to track her to the U.S., but it was a big country.

She'd been sending vague updates to her family through Kristen so they knew she was okay, and the press and citizens had been told she was overseas studying. In retrospect, the plan had several flaws, not least of which was that she couldn't be "overseas studying" for the rest of her life. But she'd been panicking and grieving when she'd made the plan and couldn't see a way out now it was in place.

She'd worried that she'd put Kristen's job in jeopardy, but her friend had assured her that her job was probably the safest of anyone's in the patrol. The queen needed Kristen right where she was in case Jenna needed specialized help, and to keep the updates coming.

As the truck turned a corner in the driveway and drove out of sight, she closed the door and picked Meg up.

"Shall we see what goodies were delivered for Bonnie?" she asked. Meg gurgled in reply and Jenna kissed the top of her head.

Liam came across the back patio, toed off his shoes at the door and waved to her through the open living areas that connected the front door to the back.

"Was that the baby supplies arriving?"

"Yes. They assembled the furniture so we just need to put it into position and bring the other pieces into the nurseries."

"We can do that now if you want," he said, resting his hands low on his hips.

"Bonnie's still asleep in your room, so it would be good timing."

They spent twenty minutes moving an extra chest of drawers into Meg's nursery and a single bed out of Bonnie's to make way for the new crib. Once they were done, they sat on the rug on the floor in Bonnie's nursery, Meg playing with a stuffed velvet frog that had been in the delivery, Liam taking sheets, blankets and baby clothes out of their plastic packets and Jenna unpacking the baby creams and lotions and setting them up on the new changing table.

Liam's deep voice broke the silence. "Is your accent Danish?"

She hesitated. Was telling him her true homeland risky? She'd been telling people she was Danish, just on the off chance they'd seen a photo of her before and the name of her country jogged their memory. But for some reason she didn't want to lie to Liam Hawke any more than it was necessary. Perhaps because he was trusting her with his daughter—the ultimate act for a parent—she felt that she'd be betraying him somehow with a lie she could avoid.

"I'm from Larsland. It's an archipelago of islands in the Baltic Sea. We're not far from Denmark and people often get our accents mixed up."

"I've heard of it. Lots of bears and otters."

"That's us," she said, smiling.

He fixed his deep green gaze on her. "Are you going home soon, or are you going to put down roots in the U.S.?"

"I'm seeing a bit of the world, so I'll probably move on at some point." That wasn't strictly true—she wasn't traveling, but she didn't yet know what the future held. Once she worked out how, she'd have to return to Larsland and face the music, and it was only fair Liam knew there was an element of uncertainty in her future. "But not until you and Bonnie are ready," she said to reassure him she wasn't flighty.

"This wasn't a lifelong commitment," he said. "As long as you give me notice, you'll be free to move on and see more of the world any time you want."

"Thanks," she said.

Liam stood, drawing her eyes up his tall frame. "I was serious when I said I'd increase your salary by twenty percent over what Dylan was paying you. And if you have any conditions, let me know."

"You don't even know if I'll be good at the job yet," she said, pushing to her feet before she got a crick in her neck.

Liam crossed his arms over his broad chest and rocked back on his heels, and once again he looked like the multi-millionaire businessman that he was. "Dylan wouldn't have kept you this long if you weren't a good worker, and Bonnie has been happy with you so far. Besides," he said with a lazy grin, "if it's not working out, I'll fire you and hire someone else."

She knew that grin was meant to soften his words. Instead, as it spread across his face, it stole her breath away. Boys and then men had tried a lot of tricks over the years to get her attention, hoping to marry into the royal family, but she'd always seen through them and been far from impressed. Yet Liam Hawke threw one careless grin her way, and she was practically putty in his hands. She held back a groan. This was not a good start to a new job....

"In the meantime," she said, bringing her focus back

to their conversation, "you want me to be happy in my work conditions on the chance I am actually good at the job."

He tilted his head in acknowledgment. "Exactly. A good businessman keeps his options open, utilizes the resources available and moves on when it's no longer effective or profitable."

Meg yawned again. "I'd better feed Meg and get her down for a nap because I think Bonnie will be awake soon."

She ran a fingertip across her daughter's button nose. Her eyes were getting heavy, so Jenna began softly humming an old Larsland lullaby that Meg liked.

Liam dug his hands into his pockets and turned to the door. "I'll leave you to it."

Without losing her place in the song or lifting her head, Jenna nodded. But once he was gone, she moved to the window so she could watch her new employer as he strode from the house toward the flower farm around back. And the question played over and over in her mind—why did she have to find this man, of all men, so appealing?

Three

Liam clawed his way through the nightmare. A child was crying, desperate, inconsolable, wanting—no *needing*—him to do something. He woke with a start, wrenching himself from the grip of the dream. Except the crying didn't stop. For a moment he didn't understand…and then it all came back.

Bonnie. His daughter was crying.

He stumbled out of bed, rubbing his face with one hand and checking he was wearing pajama bottoms with the other. Sharing night feeds with a woman meant making sure he was dressed twenty-four hours a day. He flicked on a light and saw the time—two a.m.—as he headed down the hall.

Just before he stepped into Bonnie's nursery, a light came on in the room and he saw Jenna, eyes soft with recent sleep, hair messed from her pillow and a white cotton robe pulled tightly around her body. She reached down and lifted his daughter into her arms as she whispered soothing words. Liam's heart caught in the middle of his throat, and for a long moment he couldn't breathe. The image in the soft light of the lamp was like a master's watercolor. The ethereal beauty of Jenna, her expression of love freely given to his daughter, and Bonnie's complete trust in return, was almost too much to bear. He couldn't tear his gaze away.

Jenna glanced over and gave him a sleepy smile as she soothed Bonnie, and he felt the air in the room change, felt his skin heat.

Bonnie's crying eased a little and Jenna said over her head, "She's hungry. Do you want to hold her while I make up a bottle?"

He cleared his throat and stepped closer. "Sure."

Jenna's fingers brushed the bare skin of his chest as she laid Bonnie in the crook of his elbow. The urge to hold Jenna's hand there, against his skin, was overpowering. He stood stock-still, not trusting himself to move. One thing was apparent—pajama bottoms weren't enough. For future feeds he'd have to minimize skin contact by making sure he also was wearing a shirt.

She gave Bonnie a little pat on the arm, then moved through the door and down the stairs. He followed, mesmerized by the gentle sway of her hips under her thin, white robe, but he purposefully drew his attention back to where it should be—the baby in his arms.

Stroking his crying daughter's arms in the same soothing motion Jenna had used, he followed Jenna into the kitchen and waited while she made up a bottle. She worked smoothly in his kitchen, as if she'd done this a hundred times before. Of course, she must have done exactly that for her own child. Had anyone else ever watched her and thought it was seductive? Her movements were simple, efficient, but with such natural grace it was almost as if she were dancing.

He was losing his focus again, damn it.

Was it the intimacy of the night that caused his reaction to his nanny? Normally the only women he saw at two o'clock in the morning—especially ones with sleep-tousled hair—were women he was involved with. Not that he often saw them here in his house. He preferred liaisons that didn't have too much of an impact on his personal life or intrude into his personal space. Dylan had once pointed out that Liam's philosophy was emotionally cold, but that had never bothered him—he wasn't naïve enough to think the women he dated were looking for emotional fulfillment or promises of forever.

Besides, women weren't interested in the real him, the man who was passionate about science and breeding new, unusual flowers, the man who had no time for the trappings of wealth beyond the security it could provide his family.

His oldest brother Adam had suggested that Liam had turned it into a self-fulfilling prophecy by choosing women he knew were attracted to him for his money or his looks, keeping things superficial and ending relationships before he allowed himself to be emotionally invested. Liam had ignored his brother—he was perfectly happy with things as they were. He'd never wake up to find he'd let his guard down and he'd fallen in love with someone who was using him for his wealth or had been merely entertaining herself with some twisted game the women he knew always seemed to be playing.

He leaned back against the counter and raised an impatient Bonnie to his shoulder. "Shh," he whispered. "It won't be long now."

He wasn't sure what game Bonnie's mother had been

playing. Her family was wealthy so she hadn't needed his money, but the very fact that she hadn't told him that she was pregnant showed she hadn't been a woman he could have trusted.

"Okay, sweetheart," Jenna said, turning her blue, blue gaze back to them. "Your bottle is ready. How about we go back to your lovely armchair to have it?"

She stroked her fingertips across Bonnie's head as she passed on her way to the hallway, and suddenly— and against all his advice to himself—Liam was in the ridiculous position of being jealous of a baby.

Warm bottle in her hand, Jenna rubbed her scratchy eyes and walked down the second-story hallway. Even though it hadn't been long since Meg had started sleeping through the night, she'd forgotten how demanding night feeds were.

As she reached Bonnie's nursery, she paused and asked over her shoulder, "Would you like to feed her or shall I?"

Liam cleared his throat. "You do this one. I'm still watching your technique with these things."

She nodded and settled into the armchair. She understood. Liam didn't strike her as the jump-in-with-two-feet sort of man—he was a scientist. He'd want to gather all the information first so he'd be best placed to succeed when he did attempt something new. She'd felt his gaze on her in the kitchen as if he were trying to memorize the method of preparing his daughter's bottle. Having the gorgeous Liam Hawke watch her every move was…unsettling, but obviously it would be part of the job as she taught him the skills to look after his baby and helped him bond with her. Surely she'd get used to it with time. A shiver ran up her spine, but she ignored it.

"You can pass her over now," she said, keeping her voice even.

As he leaned down, his bare chest came within inches of her face, and the scent of his skin washed over her. She took a deep breath to steady herself, but that only intensified the effect, leaving her lightheaded. Thankfully, he didn't linger as he deposited the squirming weight of Bonnie into her arms and stepped away.

As soon as Jenna gave the baby the bottle, she stopped flailing, all her energy focused on drinking. Jenna couldn't contain the smile as she took in the sheer perfection of this tiny girl.

Liam was silent for long moments, then he crossed his arms over that naked chest. "How are you finding motherhood?"

Such a loaded question. Thinking of Meg when she was Bonnie's age, Jenna lifted the baby a little higher and breathed in her newborn scent, then murmured, "It's more than I expected."

"More in what way?" His voice was low, curious.

"In every way," she said. "It's more challenging and more wondrous than I'd ever expected."

He leaned a hip against the chest of drawers. "Does Meg's father help?"

"No," she said carefully. "Her father's not on the scene."

He cocked his head to the side, his attention firmly focused on her now, not Bonnie. "Do you have family nearby to help?"

"It's really just me and Meg." Her pulse picked up speed at the half-truth, and she cast around for a new topic before she spilled all her secrets to this man in the quiet of the night. "So Bonnie's mother really didn't tell you she was pregnant?"

He scrubbed a hand down his face, and then looked out the window into the inky night. "I had no idea until I got the call from the hospital. Rebecca and I had broken up eight months ago and hadn't been in contact since. The next thing I knew, the hospital was calling to tell me that my ex-girlfriend had given birth to our daughter a couple of days ago and that Rebecca wasn't in a good way and was asking for me. But before we got to the hospital, she had passed away. They showed me Bonnie—" he cleared his throat "I took one look at her and…couldn't walk away. I'm sure you understand," he said gruffly.

Her mind overflowing with memories of her own, Jenna looked down at the baby who had caused such a reaction in Liam. "There's nothing quite as powerful as the trusting gaze of a newborn."

"Yes, that's it," he said, turning to face her, "along with knowing I'm the only parent she has left. I'm hers. And Bonnie is mine."

"That's a beautiful thing to say," she said, smiling up at him. It was true—as a single mother, she knew something of the challenges that lay ahead for him, but if he wanted his daughter, truly wanted her as it appeared that he did, then Bonnie was lucky.

"And now I have sole custody of a three-day-old baby." He speared his fingers through his already disheveled hair. "It still feels surreal. Yet the proof is currently in your arms."

"Oh, she's definitely real." Jenna smiled at him then transferred her gaze to Bonnie. "Aren't you, sweetheart?"

"It's a strange thing," he said, his voice far away,

"but the idea terrifies me, yet at the same time fills me with so much awe that I don't know what to do with it."

She knew that juxtaposition of fear and joy. Since she'd given birth to Meg, she knew it well.

Bonnie had finished the bottle, so she handed it to Liam, then lifted her against her shoulder and gently patted her back.

"What about Rebecca's family?" she asked. "Will they be involved in her life?"

He tapped his fingers against the empty bottle in a rapid rhythm. "When I was at the hospital, I met Rebecca's parents for the first time. They weren't happy to meet me." His expression showed that was an understatement.

"You hadn't met them when you were dating Rebecca?" She'd always been intrigued about how couples navigated the issue of each other's families when those families didn't include the reigning monarch of the country. She'd assumed—perhaps wrongly—it was much simpler for regular people.

He shrugged one shoulder. "We were only together a few months, and we hadn't been serious enough to meet each other's families. Apparently she'd been living with her parents while she was pregnant and had planned to take the baby back there after the birth," he said casually. Almost too casually. "They were going to help her raise my daughter."

"Without you?" Every day she wished Alexander had lived—for so many reasons, but most importantly so Meg could have met and known him. What mother would deliberately deny her child the love of its own father?

"My name was on the birth certificate, so I have to believe she was going to tell me at some point." But he said the words through a tight jaw. "And she did ask the staff to call me when she realized something was wrong, much to her parents' annoyance."

Watching the banked emotion in his eyes, Jenna put two and two together. "They're not happy that Bonnie is with you."

He let out a humorless laugh. "You could say that. In fact, I've already had a call from their lawyer about a custody suit they plan to file."

"The poor darling." Jenna brought Bonnie back down to lie in her arms and looked at her sweet little face. "To have already lost her mother, and now someone's trying to deny her a father."

"They won't win," he said, his spine straight and resolute. "My lawyer is dealing with it. Bonnie is mine. No one will take her away."

And seeing the determination etched in his every feature, she had no trouble believing him.

The next morning, Jenna tucked both babies into the new double stroller and set out to explore the gardens behind the house. The call of the outdoors was irresistible once the sun was shining. Besides, she was feeling restless.

After Bonnie's night feedings, she'd had difficulty falling asleep. Visions of the expanse of smooth skin on Liam's torso had tormented her. Memories of the crisp, dark hair scattered over his chest had dared her to reach out and test the feel under her fingertips the next time he was near. Which would be wrong on many levels, starting with Liam being her boss. She grimaced. She hadn't held many jobs—this was only her second paid position—but even she knew that making a pass at your employer wasn't the path to job security.

Beyond the patio, a small patch of green grass was hedged by a plant with glossy leaves, and beyond that, rows and rows of flowers stretched. Bright yellows, deep purples, vibrant pinks. So much color that it made her heart swell. Workers in wide-brimmed hats were dotted among the rows, and off to the side was a large greenhouse.

As they moved through a gap in the hedge onto a paved walkway, Meg squealed and reached her little hand out toward the nursery before them.

"That's where we're headed, honey," Jenna said to her daughter. "To see all the pretty flowers."

She'd known Hawke's Blooms had a large flower farm that produced much of the stock they sold in their state-wide chain of flower shops—and sent weekly deliveries to Dylan's apartment that she used to arrange—but seeing it in person was another thing entirely. It was as if she'd been watching the world in black and white when suddenly someone had flipped the switch to full Technicolor brilliance.

She pushed the stroller through the gate in the chain-mail fence that surrounded the whole farm and along the front of the rows, stopping at the top of each one to see what was growing there, bending an occasional flower over for Meg to smell. They hadn't made much progress when she caught sight of Liam making quick progress toward her from the greenhouse.

"Good morning," she said as he neared them. "We missed you at breakfast today."

"Morning." He nodded, his face inscrutable. "I wanted to get an early start to catch up on some work."

She took a deep breath of air fragranced with flowers and freshly turned earth. If she worked somewhere like this she'd probably be eager to start her days too.

"It's beautiful out here. Meg and Bonnie seem to love it already."

His eyes softened as he reached down to stroke each baby's cheek with a finger. "It's not a bad place to work."

She lifted Bonnie from the stroller and placed a delicate kiss on her downy head. "What do you think?" Jenna whispered. Bonnie's huge eyes fixed on Jenna's face, then as Liam came near, they settled on her father. "Do you want to hold her?" Jenna asked him, her heartbeat uneven from his closeness.

"Yeah, I do." He took his daughter and held her up for a long moment before murmuring, "Hello, Princess." Then he tucked her into the crook of his arm. "Thanks for bringing her out."

"No problem," she said, trying not to react to Liam using "princess" as a term of endearment for his daughter. To cover any reaction, she lifted Meg up onto her hip and asked, "Do you work out here in the gardens?"

"I come out to check on things occasionally, and sometimes I'm in the second greenhouse where we do the propagating, but mostly I work over there." He pointed to a long white building that looked more like an industrial complex than a gardening structure.

"What happens there?"

"The most interesting aspect of the entire business," he said with a grin. "Research."

Enthusiasm sparked in his eyes and she wanted to know more about what it was that made him happy, about what made this man tick. "Better ways to grow things?"

"We have people who work on that, but I prefer the plant and flower development side of things."

"Creating new flowers?" she said, hearing the touch of awe in her voice.

"Basically. Sometimes it's taking an old favorite and producing it in a new color. Or combining two flowers to create a brand-new one."

She tilted her head to the side and regarded him. "So really you're a farmer."

"No, I'm a scientist," he said in a tone that made it clear there was no doubt on this subject. "Though my parents were vegetable farmers before they moved here and started this business, and they always saw themselves as farmers."

She looked him over. His pants were neat and pressed, albeit with dirt smudges on the thighs. And his shirt was buttoned almost to the top, though there was no tie. There was definitely an aspect of "scientist in the field" about him. Which made her wonder about how he ended up here.

She switched Meg to her other hip to accommodate her daughter leaning toward Bonnie. "Did you always want to join the family business?"

"When we were young, we didn't have a choice. The business put food on the table, so we all helped. Dylan was a charmer even back then, and Adam always had an eye for a profit, so they usually manned the flower stall with Mom on weekends, and I helped Dad in the garden—digging, planting, grafting."

She chuckled. "Sounds like your brothers got the easier end of the deal."

"No, but I made sure they thought that." He shaded his eyes with his free hand as he looked out over the gardens, maybe seeing them as they once were, not as they were now. "I loved those days. Dad teaching me to graft, then leaving me alone with a shed full of plants to experiment. And once he realized I could create new flowers, things no one had seen before, he gave me room to experiment even more."

"Actually, that does sound pretty fun." She glanced down at a nearby row of red poppies and, suddenly wanted to sink her fingers into the rich earth and do a bit of gardening herself.

Following her gaze, he crouched down to the poppies, barely jostling Bonnie. He picked a single poppy with two fingers and handed it to Meg, who squealed with glee. "And," he said, still watching Meg, "there's nothing quite like the satisfaction of creating something with your own hands and knowing that it will contribute to keeping your family clothed and fed."

She could see him as a young teenager, focused on his experiments, carefully tending to the plants and recording the data in a spreadsheet. She smiled at the thought. "I'm guessing you were the serious one when you were kids."

"Adam was pretty serious too. It was usually Dylan leading us astray," he said, the corner of his mouth kicking up in a smile.

Having worked for Dylan for just over a year and watched him interacting with people, she could well believe that. Dylan Hawke had more than his fair share of persuasive charisma, and one day it would catch up with him.

Bonnie whimpered and flailed her arms, causing Liam to look from baby to nanny and back again. Without missing a beat, Jenna tucked Meg in the stroller and took Bonnie from her father as she asked, "So, have you worked here since you left school?"

Liam put his hands low on his hips, then dug them into his pockets, as if not sure what to do with them now. "I got a bachelor of science but kept my hand in here part-time. A double major in biology and genetics helped me with the development of new flowers."

"I think it's marvelous what your family has achieved here. What you've achieved here, Liam." He and his family had taken their destiny in their own hands. Until she'd left Larsland, she'd been on a course mapped out for her by others, and even now, she wouldn't trade having Meg for anything but she wasn't on a path she would have chosen if she hadn't gotten herself into a tangle. Liam was exactly where he wanted to be, doing exactly what he wanted to do. She admired that. "Thank you for sharing the story with me. It's amazing."

He shrugged. "Everyone's story is amazing if you take the time to listen. Take you, for example. You grew up on the other side of the world and now you're here. That's interesting."

Her heart skipped a beat. It was an invitation to share, and in that moment, she wanted nothing more than to tell him about her homeland, the beauty of a long summer sunset, how the winter's snow left a blanket across ages-old stone buildings or that the majesty of the Baltic Sea skirted the edges of her former world. But she couldn't. One slip and her whole story could come tumbling out. And then all the effort to create her new life would have been for nothing.

She leaned down and ran her hand over Meg's blond curls, not meeting Liam's eyes. "I really need to get Bonnie back inside for a bottle," she said as casually as she could manage. "It's been lovely being out here. Thank you."

Four

Five nights later, Liam arrived home just after eight o'clock, feeling an uneasy blend of anticipation and trepidation.

He'd always been something of a workaholic, staying up till all hours with his research, occasionally forgetting meals. And now he had an even bigger reason to ensure the productivity of Hawke's Blooms—Bonnie's future. He'd found her a good nanny, so now the best thing he could do for his daughter was make sure she'd always be financially secure.

Though, if he were honest, this evening's reluctance to come home early may have been more about gaining some distance from his newest employee. Four nights of sitting with Jenna while she attended to the night feedings in the intimacy of the silent, darkened house had led to four nights of lying awake, thinking of the woman a few doors down. Forbidden thoughts rising and swirling through his mind.

Of her mouth.

Her hands.

Her body.

Even though he knew she always dressed sensibly in her robe, the knowledge that she'd gotten up from her bed to attend to his daughter was proving to be alluring.

Yesterday it had become worse. The thoughts had leaked into his daytime activities, and visions of Jenna's skin, smooth and creamy, had distracted him from slicing the root of a plant he was grafting and he'd slipped and cut this thumb. An amateur mistake, and he'd been disgusted with himself.

He'd already been taking earlier breakfasts and ducking out of the house before Jenna woke each morning on the out of sight, out of mind theory. Today he'd taken it a step further; when he'd seen her strolling through the rows of blooms with the babies, he hadn't gone out to say hello, undermining their fledgling routine. But it wasn't just about him trying to regain control of his thoughts. This was also about Jenna.

He refused to jeopardize their arrangement by letting her know where his mind had strayed. If she guessed, she'd be uncomfortable living in his house, and he wouldn't risk her leaving for a less complicated job. Bonnie was his priority.

Not to mention that he was still a little uneasy about how quickly she'd left the other day as soon as he'd mentioned her background. If he wasn't mistaken, she'd used the excuse of Bonnie needing a feeding to avoid talking about her life. It sat uncomfortably in his gut that the woman taking care of his daughter might be hiding something, but he'd tried to dismiss it. There was probably a reasonable explanation. Though, to prove it to himself, he'd make sure he asked her about her childhood again.

Fifteen minutes ago, he'd called to tell Katherine he was on his way up to the house, and she'd said Bonnie was sleeping and dinner would be on the table when he got there. He dropped his briefcase in the living room and headed down the hall. With each step, he braced himself for the sight of Jenna.

So what if he was attracted to her? It was a simple case of mind over matter. His mind was infinitely stronger than anything his body felt.

Three steps from the dining room and he was a rock—wind and rain might pound at his surface, but nothing affected him. Two steps—solid stone, unwavering for anyone or anything. One step—he was impervious. He reached the door and walked through with a straight spine and head held high. Jenna stood gently rocking an old-fashioned white cradle that was set up near the dining table. The soft lighting made her eyes look enormous and her skin glow.

She's just a woman.

A woman of serene beauty, sure. But a woman just the same.

He paused to ensure his breathing was regular, his heartbeat even. He was a rock. Unyielding to outside influences.

He paused by the cradle. Bonnie's long lashes rested on her cheeks and he allowed himself a moment of tenderness as he watched her little chest rise and fall, her mouth move. Then he pulled himself back together and pasted on a polite smile for his employee.

"Good evening, Jenna." He pulled a chair out for her and waited.

"Hello, Liam." She took the seat and he pushed it in, careful not to touch her, as she sat down.

See? Easy. Now that he was over his initial reactions, he'd be fine. As the old saying went, familiarity breeds contempt, and though he didn't want or expect to hold Jenna in contempt, he did expect familiarity would breed indifference to her allure. It was practically scientific.

Several silver dishes with domed covers sat on the table. He lifted the cover off the first, revealing a fragrant curry. He passed the serving spoon to Jenna so she could put some on her plate.

"I'm sorry I'm late," he said, scooping rice from a second dish. "I hope it didn't put you out."

She didn't look up as she filled her plate with the food. "Not at all. It gave me a chance to talk to Katherine."

"How's that going?" Ideally, the two members of his household staff would have a good working relationship, but knowing his housekeeper and her preference for working alone, he was aware that was unlikely.

"I don't think Katherine approves of me eating with you." Her voice, normally lyrical with her Nordic accent, was somber, more careful. "I'm pretty sure she'd like to serve me in the kitchen."

"She's always been a stickler for propriety," he said in an attempt to soothe the waters.

"I'm more than happy to—"

"No. You're welcome at this table. I used to eat while reading journals or research papers, but now that I have Bonnie, it's time I started some new routines, like family dinner time. I want the tradition to be in place by the time Bonnie notices it. I told Katherine she's welcome, too, but she said she'd rather eat in her room."

Jenna ate another mouthful of curry before continuing. "Katherine will probably tell you herself, but she's hired a part-time maid to do the babies' washing and give her some support now she has a busier house."

"Good," he said and nodded. "I didn't want any of that falling to you when you're exhausted from keeping up with night feedings and looking after both girls."

Jenna settled her unflinching blue gaze on him. "You must be exhausted too. You've been getting up during the night and still going to work every day."

"Coffee has become my friend." She was right, but he wouldn't change a thing—Bonnie was worth it. He glanced over at the cradle, wishing his daughter was awake so he could hold her. Yet, even if she were awake, she'd prefer Jenna to him. His stomach hollowed and he turned back to his plate. "How was Bonnie this evening?"

"She cried a bit and didn't want to settle. I brought the cradle in here and had her with me while I made out the grocery order for Katherine, and she was happier with that until she drifted off." Jenna took the dish of spicy lentils that he passed and spooned some onto her plate. "Will you have any time free tomorrow? I'd like to start working on your bonding with Bonnie as soon as possible."

"Tomorrow will be difficult. What about tonight?" Creating a relationship with his daughter was a priority, but he also had to be careful about his work now that he was providing for a daughter. It was not the time to let things slip.

"That could work." She checked her watch. "She'll probably be awake for another feeding in less than an hour. We can do something then."

"Sounds good."

She spooned some more curry onto her plate. "Have you heard anything from Bonnie's mother's family? Are they still planning on filing for custody?"

"They've already taken the preliminary steps." In fact, they were becoming a royal pain in his butt. "My lawyer is on it and he doesn't think they stand a chance."

She nodded and looked back down at her plate. He took a mouthful of dhal and they ate for several minutes in silence. He and Jenna didn't know each other well, and conversation was hard to create. He wasn't good at small talk. Dylan was always telling him he needed to improve his ability to chat when they attended business functions or charity events. He drew in a breath. Now was as good a time as any. Plus, he could quiz Jenna about her background again.

"You asked me a few days ago what I wanted to be when I grew up, and I've been wondering the same about you." He picked up his water glass, took a sip and then watched her over the rim.

She bit down on her lip and looked at her plate for a long moment before replying. "Liam, if it's all the same to you, I'd rather not talk about my childhood."

He sat back in his chair and swirled the water in his glass. Interesting. Perhaps she had a difficult time growing up and preferred not to think about it. Or perhaps she was keeping a secret. He couldn't force her to answer questions, but he would wait for the right moment to push further.

If she was hiding something, he'd find out what it was.

No one had ever asked her what she'd wanted to be—not as an adult or as a child. She was a princess. A princess with four older siblings would never be queen, but she was still expected to dedicate her life to her people. Her three brothers had served in the military, but that was about as far as the children of the monarch could move away from their royal duties.

Mewling from the cradle let them know Bonnie was waking. Jenna jumped up, eager for the distraction. "You keep her entertained, and I'll make her bottle."

She saw his quick doubtful glance at the cradle and suppressed a smile. He'd held Bonnie often but usually when she was fed and happy. And quiet.

When Jenna came back into the room with a warm bottle, Liam was sitting at the table, looking bemused as he held a screaming Bonnie. When he spotted her, the relief on his face was almost comical. "Thank goodness. She's been telling me that she's pretty desperate."

"At full volume." Jenna chuckled, took Bonnie from him and sat back in her own chair. "It's all right, little one. I have your bottle right here."

As she fed the baby, Liam finished his dinner, though she felt his steady gaze on her the whole time.

"Want me to take her so you can finish your meal?" he said when Bonnie was done.

"That would be great, thanks." She handed him the now happy baby. As Jenna resumed eating, she sneaked glances at man and daughter. The soft, loving expression on his face when he looked down at his baby turned her heart to putty.

In her world, men didn't have much to do with babies—there were nannies for that. Liam's murmured words, his stroking of her tiny cheeks, affected Jenna more than she would have guessed and made her grieve the loss of a father for Meg all over again. Her own little girl was missing out on this.

It also made her miss her own father and mother. It

had been more than a year since she'd seen them, since she'd heard their voices. This job with Liam would need to be her last in the States—soon, she'd have to work out a plan to return home. It still seemed impossible, but she had to believe that when the time came, she'd find the right way.

When she'd finished her meal, Liam returned Bonnie to the cradle so they could clear the plates, then stood with his hands resting on his hips. "So what's your plan for me with Bonnie tonight?"

She'd been mulling over that very question in her mind all day. Where to start was important. "I was thinking we could try you and Bonnie with her baby carrier."

"Baby carrier?" He rubbed a hand across his raspy chin. "I thought you'd have us doing something more…"

"Hands-on?" She reached for the gray and white carrier she'd slipped behind the cradle to have it accessible.

He shrugged a shoulder. "Yes, actually."

"If we fit the carrier straps to your size and you're comfortable in it, it will give you a certain amount of independence with her. You'll be able to duck in and pick her up during the day if you want, and you'll have your hands free. The easier that becomes, the more time you'll be able to spend with her."

"And the more time I spend with her, the stronger our bond. Got it. Hear that, Bonnie?" The baby was lying back in her cradle, her little arms flailing as she watched them. "This is the first step to our new bond."

Jenna gave the cotton and mesh a shake. "If you're ready, the first thing we need to adjust the carrier straps to fit you."

He looked dubiously at the contraption in her hand. "Is it the right size?"

"They come in one size and we adjust it." She length-ened the strap, then reached up to loop it over his head but hesitated. She'd done this countless times on herself, but pulling it over Liam's thick mahogany hair seemed an act of intimacy that was beyond the boundaries of their relationship.

"Er, you might be a bit tall for me to reach...." It was an obvious lie. He was taller, yes, but if he ducked his head there was no reason she couldn't manage the task. She held the carrier out to him, and Liam seemed to take her assessment at face value.

He took the carrier and slipped it over his head and threaded his arms through, then held the pouch section out in front of him. "This will hold her?"

"She'll be well supported." The carrier needed to be a little tighter so that Liam could hold Bonnie more firmly against his chest, but the threaded buckle was at the back, so it would be awkward for him to do it himself. Perhaps Jenna should have asked Katherine to help with this part. "If you turn around, I'll adjust it."

Suddenly she was presented with the expanse of pale blue shirt fabric pulled firmly across his broad shoulders. A prickle of heat raced across her skin. She wanted to allow her hands to roam, to trace the shape of him under the material, to luxuriate in the warm solidness of him.

He didn't move—patiently waiting for her to help him with something for his daughter. Which was enough to snap Jenna out of the mood that had descended. Quickly, she tightened the straps to fit firmly around him, ignoring the exquisite torture of her fingers brushing against him.

"Okay, I think that's about right," she said brightly. "I'll pop Bonnie in, and check the fitting again then."

As he turned back around, Jenna picked Bonnie up, gave her a quick kiss on the cheek and slid her into the pouch strapped to her father's chest. Bonnie's neck arched against the head support and she locked her gaze on her father's face.

"I think she likes it already," Jenna said.

Liam put a hand up behind Bonnie's head, as he examined as much of the carrier as he could see, as if making an assessment about its construction and the safety of his daughter. "I thought I'd seen babies facing the other way."

"As she gets a bit older, we can adjust it and have her facing forward. Older babies like to see the world, but right now she'd rather be snug against you."

Liam whispered something to Bonnie, and Jenna saw his Adam's apple move slowly up and down. Tears of tender emotion pressed at the back of her eyes, but she blinked them away and busied herself reading the instruction leaflet that came with the carrier, despite having read it several times already, and allowed father and daughter to have their moment.

"Did you wear one of these much with Meg?" he finally asked, glancing up.

Jenna smiled as she circled him, testing the straps and the fit. "She practically lived in one. After work, I was busy trying to get our washing and cooking done. But I hadn't seen her all day, so I didn't want to be apart from her either."

He nodded in understanding. "And with the carrier, you could do both things at once."

"In theory," she said wryly. "Often I'd get distracted by Meg and end up with no washing or cooking done and I'd eat a banana for dinner."

She felt the low rumble of his laugh as it vibrated

through his chest and quickly dropped her hands. "I think she's safe and snug in there," she said, stepping back. "How does it feel?"

He leaned a fraction to one side, then the other and swiveled at the waist, as if testing the carrier's scope. "It's surprisingly comfortable. I mean, I know she's there and my center of gravity is different, but I'd expected it to feel more cumbersome."

"That's great. Why don't you take a walk through the house? See if it feels secure while you move around."

He wandered off, ambling from room to room, leaving her watching him. But she felt more like a voyeur than someone supervising the process. His body moved with such masculine grace, and the carrier straps emphasized the set of his shoulders.

Her heart clenched tight. Why was she having such inappropriate thoughts about her boss? And, maybe more important, why was she so ineffective at controlling them?

She sank into the dining chair and covered her face with her hands, forced to acknowledge that she was quite possibly in over her head.

Two days later, Liam met Jenna and the babies at the door to his research facility. On a whim—one he was still struggling to understand—he'd sent a note to the house inviting them down to see where he worked.

"Hi, Liam," Jenna said brightly. "Thanks for the invitation." She'd worn a summer dress and an orange wide-brimmed hat, and for a moment he felt a pang at not being able to see her silky blond hair.

"Hi," he said, looking at the double stroller. "It might be better if we carry them. And you won't need your hat in here either." He slipped off his white lab coat, threw it over one arm and scooped Meg up in the other. Meg was the heavier of the babies, so he'd instinctively reached for her to save Jenna's arms, but he'd surprised himself lately by liking Meg in his arms almost as much as Bonnie. She had such a sweet personality even at this young age.

Jenna picked Bonnie up and followed him through the doors.

"I'm glad you could make it," he said as they walked down a corridor.

"We wouldn't have missed a personal tour for anything, would we, girls?" Meg gurgled in his arms at her mother's voice.

Beyond family and his research staff, he'd never allowed anyone into his rooms. Corporate espionage was always a concern—if there was a flower he'd developed and was about to patent, a competitor would love the opportunity to see it and try to trump him.

But there was a personal element too.

Since the day his father had given him a plot of land and free rein to breed his own flowers when he was fifteen, he'd always grown his plants with a fair amount of privacy. He had staff to help now, to carry out tasks such as replicating his experiments to ensure the plants would throw the same flower every time and that the cultivars were healthy. But, in his own lab on a day-to-day basis, he still worked alone. It was a more personal space to him than his home.

So why he'd invited Jenna Peters into his inner sanctum was anyone's guess. He inwardly winced. He could rationalize it and say he was letting his daughter visit him at work—something he hoped she would continue to do as she got older—and she needed her nanny to bring her, but he knew that wasn't the truth.

There was something about Jenna that he trusted. Sure she'd been reluctant to talk about her childhood when asked, but he'd decided it must be painful for her. She simply wasn't the type of person to hide anything from him.

As they walked down the sterile white corridor past rooms filled with activity, a few of his staff rushed over to coo over the two babies, but even those who didn't watched his progress. Having non-research or admin staff in the building was enough of a surprise to raise eyebrows, but his personal assistant had told him that his instant fatherhood had been a hot topic of gossip among the staff, so he was sure the rumor mill had filled everyone in on whose baby was in the nanny's arms. He found he didn't mind the extra attention as much as he usually did.

They passed through a set of double doors into the area where he worked. Usually he was the only one in these rooms unless he called on an assistant to lend a hand. His heart rate felt uneven and he realized he was uneasy, waiting for Jenna's reaction.

Jenna stood in the middle of the first room, Bonnie in her arms, and turned around in a full circle. "This is where you work, isn't it?"

His attention snapped to her. "How did you know?"

"It…" Her voice trailed off as she looked from the surroundings back to him. "This is going to sound crazy, but it feels like you in here."

"Feels like me," he repeated dubiously. He narrowed his gaze as he took in the rows and rows of seedlings that he hoped would grow up to be something special, the whiteboards covered in diagrams of the generations of the cultivars, the computers and microscopes. "I'm not sure how it 'feels' any different in this room from the other rooms we passed along the way."

"That's the crazy part." She grinned at him. "Maybe—" She leaned in and sniffed his shoulder, and Meg made a grab for her hair. "No. I was thinking maybe it smelled like your cologne in here and my subconscious picked it up, but you're not wearing any."

He tried to get his lungs working again after she'd leaned so close. "None of the staff wear cologne to work," he said, hoping his voice was normal. "We often need to smell fragrances from a flower, so we don't want outside influences floating around."

She shrugged. "I don't know what it is then. I'll keep thinking about it." She wandered over and peeked through the glass panels in the door to the next room. "What's through here?"

A small swell of pride filled his chest—this project had been his greatest success so far. "Something I've been working on."

Watching her face so he didn't miss her reaction, he opened the door and waved her through.

Five

As Jenna stepped through the doorway of Liam's laboratory, her breath caught in her throat. The windowless room had artificial lighting beaming down on rows of benches covered in small black pots that were bursting with glossy green leaves, each with the same flower on long stalks rising elegantly. It was a single, curved petal of a lily, but this bloom was darkest blue. It was stunning.

"Liam, you created this?" she asked once she'd found her voice.

He nodded. "Well, it was a joint project with Mother Nature."

"It's amazing." She walked along the benches, looking at flower after flower, each as perfect as the last. "Has anyone else seen them?"

"Just the staff here. And Adam and Dylan, so they're ready for when we release it to the public."

She couldn't stop looking at the lilies. She'd never seen anything like them. "This will create a sensation."

"Thank you," he said. "I'm hoping so."

Unable to resist, she reached out and ran a fingertip over a thick, waxy petal. "What sort of launch are you planning for it?"

"I leave that to my brothers, but Dylan's office usually has window signs made up for all the Hawke's Blooms stores when we release a new flower, and Adam's office will probably put out a press release. Gardening magazines and TV shows usually pick up on it, and occasionally we get lucky and the mainstream media mentions it."

This flower deserved more than a poster and a press release. This flower deserved fanfare and fame. "Have you ever done anything more to promote your creations?"

"What more is there?" he asked, frowning.

Her mind kicked into gear, suddenly full of possibilities. "Maybe an event. Something to really make a splash. Something that would get you a lot of publicity and make the blue lily the most sought-after flower in the state."

Liam handed Meg a rubber stress ball from his desk as he asked, "What are you thinking?"

If there was one thing Jenna knew about, it was events. She'd been attending large-scale occasions since she was a child. "It could be almost anything, like a media stunt, or maybe a snazzy release, like the way a bottle of champagne is smashed against the bow of a boat." She'd christened her first ship when she was sixteen. It was more fun than cutting a ribbon, but there was always the danger of splashing her dress. "Perhaps something elegant. How about a ball?"

"For a flower?" he asked dubiously. "People would go to that?"

"Sure they would if you promise them a good time. Make it the party of the year."

Meg reached up and grabbed a fistful of his dark, wavy hair, but Liam barely flinched. "What exactly constitutes a 'party of the year'?"

She thought back over the successful events she'd attended. "Location, guest list, entertainment, food. Just the basics, but done really well."

He arched an eyebrow. "You seem to know a lot about this sort of thing."

"I've attended a few in the past. I had a boyfriend who was often invited to big parties and events." Which was true. In her previous life, whichever guy she'd been seeing had been invited to the events she attended as her plus one.

Apparently accepting her explanation at face value, he sank into a chair in front of a messy desk and leaned back, Meg on his lap. "What else would you do?"

Good question. To start with, they'd need a theme. "Have you named the flower?"

"I was planning on calling it Midnight."

"That's perfect," she said, feeling a little buzz of adrenalin. "You could make midnight the theme of the ball. The decorations would all be in midnight blue, and maybe the official launch would be at the stroke of midnight, perhaps someone cutting a ribbon, and every guest could be given a gift and a cut Midnight Lily. Naturally, you'd make sure there was press coverage, perhaps some influential bloggers, anyone who would talk it up beforehand and afterward."

He made some notes on a jotter on his desk, then turned to her as Meg tried to grab his pen. "I'll run it past Adam and Dylan, but I think it's a great idea. Thanks."

"My pleasure." She smiled. It had been a while since she'd used her brain in that way and it was fun. "I'm sure you'll make it a success."

He ran a hand over his chin, then tapped a finger against his jaw. "Would you consider overseeing the event? You have your hands full with Bonnie and Meg, but my admin staff can put all your plans into action. It would be more about being the ideas person and giving advice about the whole thing."

Jenna chewed the inside of her cheek. The very last place she could be was a party covered by the media. If a single photo of her leaked back to her homeland, her whole plan would come crashing down around her and she'd have to return before she was ready.

"The thing is," she began, thinking on her feet, "I hate being in front of people, talking to the media, that sort of thing. And crowds. So I'm not the best person to organize it."

He shook his head, obviously not seeing her objection as an obstacle. "Adam or Dylan would do all the public speaking, and Dylan's office, which oversees the Hawke's Blooms stores, has a PR person. She can be the liaison with the media. And if you're worried about the crowds, you wouldn't even have to attend. You can be as behind the scenes as you want to be. It's your ideas I want."

A bubble of excitement filled her chest just thinking about it, and she held her breath for a beat as if that could contain it. She had heaps of accumulated knowledge about events, which was currently of no benefit to anyone. She could make use of her knowledge and help Liam and Dylan, who'd both given her a home and a job when she'd needed them.

Then again, her conscience protested, she'd never actually organized an event of this size on her own. She'd feel like a fraud. Her excitement deflated.

Reluctantly, she admitted the truth. "The best thing would be to hire an event organizer, someone with experience and training."

"True, but I've never been known for traditional hiring practices. Just look at the process of hiring my brother's housekeeper to be my nanny, and that's working out just fine. Besides," he said with a pointed look, "you're the one who convinced me that we should do it differently this time, so it's pretty much your responsibility to see that through."

She laughed at his attempt at levity. "Okay, all right. I'll give it a go, but I can't promise that I'll do it as well as a professional would."

A spark of triumph flared in his eyes, and he grinned. "You just do it your way—that's all I'll be expecting. I'll run it past Adam and Dylan and get a team together to meet with you."

A few minutes later, Jenna pushed the stroller out of the building into the brilliant sunshine and the scents of the flower farm and wondered what she'd just gotten herself into.

"Girls," she said, looking down at the two babies, "sometime soon I might need to learn to say no to Liam Hawke."

When Liam arrived home that night it was almost eleven o'clock. The house was quiet, calm. He felt an ironic smile creep across his face. A few months ago, quiet and calm had been his house's natural state. Then his daughter had arrived, bringing sunshine and happy chaos with her. Meg had only added to that.

Jenna, however, had interrupted his calm in a different way. In a wholly unexpected and unwelcome way. Even now, thinking about her, his pulse accelerated against his will.

He headed up the stairs and down the hall and noticed the light in Bonnie's nursery was on. Bonnie must be having her bottle, which was good timing—he could stop in and help with that before falling into bed. But when he reached the room, it was empty of furniture and Jenna stood with her back to him as she painted the walls daffodil yellow. In a simple white T-shirt and cut-off denim shorts stretching nicely over her rounded bottom, she was the most alluring woman he could remember seeing. His mouth was suddenly dry. He swallowed once, twice.

"Well, this is unexpected," he said, leaning on the door frame.

She whirled to face him, eyes startled and face covered in splatters of bright yellow. A large spot sat lopsided on her nose, and drips decorated her white T-shirt.

"I thought you said it was okay for me to paint this room," she said in a rush. "The dark browns—"

He held up a hand. "It's fine. You're right, I wanted the nursery redecorated—I just thought you'd get a contractor in to do it. Painting walls isn't in your job description."

She shoved some hair that had fallen from her ponytail away from her face, but it flopped back straight away. "I wanted to do it. I've never painted a room before."

He couldn't hold back the laugh—she was so earnest. "It's hardly up there with life goals like climbing Mt. Everest or touring a medieval castle."

"I suppose," she said with a secret smile dancing around her mouth, "it depends on what a person has and hasn't experienced before."

"I suppose so." He pushed off the doorframe and wandered around the room, scrutinizing her handiwork.

"It's not too bad, is it?" Her hand fluttered as she tucked the stray strand of hair behind her ears. She seemed more uncertain than she had about anything since he'd met her.

The edges were crooked in places, but given it was her first time, it looked remarkably neat. "You've done a good job."

She beamed at the simple praise as she pointed to the windowsill. "I know the edges need some work. I'll go over them when I've finished here."

"How about I change my clothes and give you a hand? I know some tricks that will make it easier." He was sure he'd regret this later, but in that moment, seeing her glowing from within, he couldn't walk away.

"Oh, no," she said emphatically. "I couldn't ask you to do that after a long day at work. I'll be fine."

"I assume you've also put in a long day already. Speaking of your job," he said mildly, "where exactly is my daughter?"

Jenna rubbed her forehead with the back of her hand, leaving another adorable smear of yellow. "Sleeping in Meg's room. I moved Meg's crib into my room until I've finished in here and Bonnie can move back in."

"Okay. I'll do a quick check on her, then change into some old clothes and be back."

He slipped out and into the room next door and saw

the perfect little face of his child. She still made his breath catch in wonder every time he saw her.

She was a miracle, and she was his. Would he ever feel worthy of her?

Jenna sighed heavily after Liam left the room. Spending time with him on a joint project sounded like sweet torture. It was hard enough being with him late at night when she fed Bonnie, but at least they had the baby to focus on and clearly defined roles. She was the nanny, awake for a night feeding.

Though, truth be told, she was often at sea in Liam's house. When she'd lived in the palace, she also had a clearly defined role—she was the daughter of the queen and she had access to certain areas, knew who worked where and how things should be. When she'd lived in Dylan's apartment as his housekeeper, she'd had her own space downstairs and clearly defined boundaries— she cleaned Dylan's living areas but she didn't spend time in them, and her own rooms were hers and private.

Yet here in this house, she was sharing Liam's personal space, despite barely knowing him, despite being his employee. Liam had encouraged her to make herself at home, but that wasn't realistic.

Could that be why she reacted to her boss as a man? The boundaries of home and work were so confused that the boundaries between the man who signed her paychecks and the man who filled out a button-down shirt like no one's business were destined to be equally as confused.

Liam strode back into the room wearing an old T-shirt that fit him perfectly and a pair of blue jeans that had become soft with washing and hung low on his hips, molding over his thighs. A low, insistent pulse beat through her body. It seemed that it wasn't just when he was wearing button-down shirts that he affected her....

"Where would you like me to start?" he asked, his voice deep and rich.

She swallowed, trying to get her voice to work. "Maybe on the edges. As you pointed out, I'm not particularly good at them."

"No one's perfect at something the first time they try it, Jenna. It takes practice." He rested his hands on his hips as he assessed the spots he'd be working on. "You've done a good job for your first time."

"That's kind of you to say," she said, feeling a blush creeping up her cheeks.

He picked up a paintbrush and dipped it in the sunshine yellow paint. "Just truth. I'm a simple black-and-white, facts-and-figures kinda guy."

She wondered if he truly believed that or if it was a throwaway line. He'd said it in all seriousness, but surely the man who'd created the Midnight Lily and taken the photographs that adorned the bedroom walls couldn't see himself as only a "facts-and-figures kinda guy"? She had so many questions about Liam Hawke.

They painted in silence for a few minutes before she found the courage to pose one of them. One she owed it to Bonnie to ask. "Can I ask you something personal?"

"You can ask," he said, his voice teasing as he crouched to reach a corner. "However, I'll reserve the right not to answer."

She paused with her roller midair, trying to get the words right. "You work such long hours. Wouldn't you prefer to spend more time with Bonnie?"

He shrugged and kept painting. "Of course I would, but I have other responsibilities too."

"You told Katherine to take on a helper because the

situation had changed," she said as politely as she could. She knew she was treading on dangerous ground, questioning her employer, but she had to say something for Bonnie's sake. "Shouldn't the same principle apply to you, so you can balance your obligations to the business with those to Bonnie?"

He reached into his pocket, brought out a roll of masking tape and began to tape around the edges of the window. "Part of the role of a father is to ensure his children have everything they need in life. I know what it's like to start out poor, and I won't let that happen to my daughter. So sometimes, yes, I need to work harder and longer so I can make sure she has every opportunity in life that I can create for her."

Taking her cue from him, Jenna kept working as she spoke, despite wanting to watch his expression. "You know, my parents prioritized their work over spending time with their children." Their work had been royal duties, but the principle was the same. "Bonnie doesn't care if her sheets are 1,500-thread count cotton or 300-thread count. She doesn't care whether she gets to use a designer diaper. She just wants the thing taken off after she's made a mess. Bonnie cares about you being there, about being held, loved, fed."

She could feel his gaze land on her. "Correct me if I'm wrong, but isn't that what I employed you for?"

"Yes and no." She moved to the next wall and kept painting. The fact they weren't looking at each other was probably making this personal topic easier to discuss. "Nannies aren't for life, and after I'm gone, Bonnie will only have you. *You* will be the constant in her life, the one whose love and attention she'll crave."

The silence on the other side of the room made her risk a quick glance at him. She caught him letting out a long breath and rubbing the back of his neck with his spare hand.

She winced, but she'd come this far, so she may as well finish what she'd started. The roller tray was nearly empty, so she tipped more paint from the can as she spoke. "You want to know what I think?"

"Shoot," he said wearily.

"I think it would be easy to hide in science," she said, choosing her words with care. "Babies and love are unpredictable and messy. Science is logical. In some ways, science would be simpler than real life."

"Science has rules. It has order." His voice was grave with the weight of conviction. "Science is measurable. Science doesn't lie."

The silence in the room was heavy, as if they both realized the depth of this accidental revelation. Part of her wanted to leave him alone, not to push on something so personal. The other part couldn't let this little window into a man who fascinated her go.

"People lie?" she asked softly.

She sneaked a glance and saw him shrug. "They've been known to."

"Like Rebecca not telling you she was pregnant?"

"That's one example," he acknowledged, his voice even. Then he shifted position to paint around the windowsill as if this wasn't a big deal.

Jenna hesitated, again torn between wanting to let him talk and not pushing. Finally, she decided to leave the decision to him. "Liam, you don't have to tell me anything. I'm just your daughter's nanny. But if you want to tell me, I'd be interested in listening."

He didn't say anything for long moments, then cleared his throat. "When I was eleven, we moved from the Midwest out here to California. I'd been in elementary school and started here in my first year of middle school. My parents thought I'd be fine—all the kids my age were in a new school, so we were all in the same boat."

"But you were in a different boat altogether," she guessed.

"I was," he acknowledged ruefully. "The kids I used to be friends with had helped out on their parents' farms after school, like we did. The kids in the new school had no responsibilities and were obsessed with labels and other status symbols."

Her heart broke a little for that boy who was a complete fish out of water, but she tried to keep the sympathy from her voice, knowing he wouldn't want it. "It sounds like you would have had culture shock."

"Perhaps I did." He added more masking tape further along the edge and went back to painting. "Then the flower farm started doing well, and our parents moved the three of us to prestigious private schools."

She grimaced, imaging what was to come. "Which was worse."

"Absolutely," he said on a humorless laugh. "Full of rich kids who were spoiled brats. Bragging and exaggerating were normal parts of conversations, and they were always playing power games. Everything came with a price. Nothing was as it seemed."

She'd met kids like that when she was young—they'd say they wanted to be her friend, but it was all about her title, not the person she was. "Self-centered and not afraid who knew it."

"That's about it." His voice wasn't bitter or accusing, simply matter-of-fact. "For a country boy, it was all so foreign. My brothers and I were unfashionably family-oriented."

"Yet, now you're probably richer than many of them," she said, knowing she was pointing out the obvious.

"There's a difference between self-made wealth and inherited wealth. People who are born to wealth and privilege are a different species."

Her heart clenched and sank. "And those born to wealth and privilege are a species you have no time for," she clarified, but his tone had been clear enough.

"It's a culture of one-upmanship. It's dishonest."

If he knew the truth about her, she'd only reinforce his theory—she had been born to wealth and privilege and her life now—even her own name—was a lie. And it mattered. For some reason Liam Hawke's opinion of her mattered way more than it should. A tight band seemed to clamp around her chest, making it difficult to draw in breath.

"You know," she said, putting down her roller, "it's quite late. I'll finish this tomorrow. Thanks for your help."

She heard a muffled groan and turned. He stretched up into standing and rubbed a hand over his eyes. If he knew she was another one of the people who lied to him, there would be disgust in his gaze. Disgust at her. How would she be able to stand that? She looked back to the roller tray.

"Jenna," he said softly.

Even knowing what he'd think of her if he knew the truth, she couldn't help turning back to him when he said her name.

"I shouldn't have laid all that on you. I'm sorry." He reached a hand out to rest on her shoulder. "It's my crap, not yours and now I've made you uncomfortable."

His nearness made her pulse race, and her shoulder tingled where his hand rested. The contrast between that excitement and the heaviness in her chest about her deception was almost too much to bear.

"No, you didn't say anything wrong. I'm just tired. Probably too many paint fumes."

"Here, I'll help you clean up," he said, turning and picking up the brushes.

Five more minutes this close to him was out of the question. She had to get some space or risk losing control, pushing him against that wall and kissing him with all the crazy, confused desire inside her. Or she might even break down and confess the secret she'd been keeping. Then he'd see her as the same as all the other people who'd lied to him. Either option was unthinkable.

She pasted on a fake smile that she knew didn't reach her eyes.

"It will only take me a minute. Really," she said, with as much conviction as she could muster. "I'll see you tomorrow."

For a long moment, he didn't move, just watched her with a frown line crossing his forehead. Then he nodded slowly. "Tomorrow." And he walked out the door.

Six

The afternoon sun streamed through the window of Bonnie's nursery, silhouetting Jenna as she painted the final touches on the newly white window frame.

She hadn't heard him, so for a moment Liam took the opportunity to watch her work, to appreciate the sheer beauty of this woman who'd so suddenly become a part of his life. A woman who made the world a little brighter wherever she was.

He must have made a sound because she started and turned. "Oh, it's you," she said in her musical accent.

"Just me." He stepped into the room. "No babies?"

She rested her brush on the side of the paint tin and rose to stretch. "Bonnie's asleep and Katherine has taken Meg for a walk."

"Katherine?" he asked, incredulous.

Jenna shrugged one shoulder, causing the pale blue cotton of her T-shirt to stretch across her breasts. "She offered. She said she could see I wanted to finish the painting, but I think she and Meg have developed a certain devotion to each other."

In the eight years Katherine had worked for either him or his parents in this house, he'd never seen her display devotion to anything other than her job. "Wonders will never cease," he said and considered whether he'd been underestimating his housekeeper.

"Don't be too surprised," Jenna said with a lopsided grin. "She still doesn't particularly like me."

He laughed as much for Jenna's self-deprecation as for the humor in the situation. "Then the universe still makes sense."

She picked up a rag and wiped her hands. "If you're just dropping in to see Bonnie, I can—"

"No," he said, interrupting her. "I'm home for the day."

Her eyes were wide when they met his. "At four o'clock?"

He dug his hands into his pockets and nodded. He'd given this a lot of thought during the day and had made a decision. "You were right last night. I've been seeing this from the wrong angle. Bonnie needs her father around. It's time I made that happen."

Jenna's blue eyes glistened, then she blinked and smiled. "She's a lucky little girl."

The pureness of the emotion in her eyes resonated through him, seemed to take hold of his heart and squeeze, and he had to clear his throat before he could reply. "I appreciate that, but we both know that as a parent, I have a long way to go."

"It takes practice," she said, repeating his words from last night.

He smiled wryly. "True. That's why I've rearranged

things at work and handed some tasks and projects over to my staff." His two senior research assistants had been surprised but keen for the extra responsibility, and he'd also talked to his PA about handing some tasks to her. "My plan is to be home by four o'clock every day."

"That's amazing, Liam. Bonnie will love having the extra time with you." She looked at him with admiration shining in her eyes, and he had to wonder if he'd partly made the decision because it was Jenna who'd suggested it. He'd like to think he'd have realized the right thing to do on his own, but he couldn't deny the effect she had on him.

He let out a long breath, wanting to respond only as a father, not a man who was having trouble focusing anywhere but on his nanny's lips.

He shrugged as casually as he could manage. "I can't promise how successful it will be, that I'll be home by four every day, but I'll definitely aim for that."

"We'll be able to work much faster on your bonding with Bonnie."

He'd been thinking about that and knew just what he wanted to do next. "I'd like to learn to feed her on my own. There's no reason we both have to get up every night."

"I've been thinking the same thing." She put the lid on the paint tin and gathered up her brushes as she spoke. "I'm sure you'll find that those late-night feedings, when it's just the two of you, can be a special time."

They probably would be. Plus, this plan had the advantage of not feeling tempted by seeing Jenna in that thin robe when he was only half awake and his defenses were low. "How soon can we start?"

"Tonight, if you're ready," she said, looking at him

with those clear blue eyes, beguiling him with those cupid's bow lips.

"That will be great." He headed for the door before he did something stupid, like kissing her here in the freshly painted nursery. "Let me know when she's ready for her next bottle."

He walked down the hall to his room, loosening his tie as he went. Now he just had to survive one more night of the temptation that was his nanny and he was home free. Well—he hesitated with his hand on the doorknob to his room—that covered the nights, but he couldn't be sure of coping with the temptation that was Jenna during the day. He threw the door open and once he was in, he leaned back and hit his head against the door behind him.

Liam spent the late afternoon hours sprawled in the living room playing with Meg and asking Jenna her opinion on topics he'd come across in the baby books he'd been reading, such as routines and when to introduce solids into Bonnie's diet. Her opinions were well considered and interesting, and he found himself simultaneously agreeing with her and thinking he should take notes. He thanked the fates he'd stumbled across someone like Jenna to care for his daughter. Their situation was ideal. Well, it would be as long as he could keep his rogue attraction to her at bay.

Dusk was settling over the landscape when Bonnie's little cries came over the baby monitor.

"That's my cue," Jenna said, unfolding herself from the sofa and heading for the stairs.

He scooped Meg up and followed. "Come on, Meg. Group trip to the nursery." The baby gurgled and babbled her agreement.

Liam walked down the hall after Jenna, trying not to watch the sway of her hips but failing. There was something very particular about the way she walked—it was almost gliding. Had she had deportment lessons as a child, perhaps?

In Meg's room—which was still temporarily Bonnie's—Jenna reached into the crib, but Liam put out a hand to stop her. "I'll do it all this time. You just talk me through it. It's the only way I'll become self-sufficient."

Jenna took Meg from him and nodded. "Okay."

Slipping his hands under the baby to support her in all the right places, he lifted her to his chest. Her little face was red and her arms flailed. "Shh," he said. "You might need a bit of patience for this, but I promise you'll get fed in the end."

Jenna sank down into the armchair with Meg, who was playing with her own toes. "First, she'll want a clean diaper," Jenna said.

He'd had some practice at changing diapers, so he was fairly confident and managed to complete the task without incident.

"Done," he said and held his diapered daughter in the air.

"She'll be perky for a little while since it's still early, so she'd probably like a bit of time on her play mat."

Play mat. Right. He looked around and nothing jumped out at him. "Where do we keep the play mat?"

"It's folded in the bottom drawer. It has a mobile that arches over the top and she loves it when you play on that with her."

He found the mat, laid it out on the carpet, put Bonnie on top and then clicked the arms of the mobile together. Bonnie seemed happy, but how, exactly, was he supposed to play with her? He wasn't a complete idiot—he'd worked out how to play with Meg, but she had more control over her limbs and a rudimentary understanding of games. Bonnie was a different matter.

He rubbed a hand over his chin. "What—?"

"The soft animals hanging from the mobile arms all make different sounds if you handle them and Bonnie loves it when you touch them for her. Try the ladybug—she's crinkly."

Liam crinkled the ladybug, then surprised himself by losing track of time as he lay on the floor playing with his daughter.

"I think she's getting tired," Jenna finally said. "She'll appreciate a bottle and a sleep."

Reluctantly Liam packed up. When he'd spent time thinking about being a father to Bonnie, he'd mainly thought of himself as a caregiver in this phase of her life and not really being able to interact with her until she was a bit older. He'd never suspected that he'd be sorry to put a play mat away.

"Right," he said, "we're ready."

Jenna stood back so he could pass her and head for the kitchen. She talked him through making up his first bottle. On the other night feedings, he'd held Bonnie while Jenna had made the milk, so the juggling act of holding a baby while carrying out the task was more of a challenge than the bottle itself.

Back in the nursery, he settled down into the armchair, bottle in one hand, his now fussy daughter in the other. "You know, they showed me how to do this at the hospital the day I met Bonnie, but I'm afraid I was so overwhelmed, I didn't pay enough attention."

"No matter. It's all worked out perfectly fine," Jenna said with a smile. "Lay her back along your forearm. And tilt the bottle to her."

Getting the bottle past those angry fists was easier said than done, but once Bonnie had the teat in her mouth, she stilled, as if all her focus was on the food. Triumph surged through him at being able to successfully feed his daughter; it satisfied something primal inside.

"Have you heard anything more from Rebecca's parents?" Jenna asked softly.

He sighed. "Our lawyers had a phone meeting today to see if they could negotiate an agreement."

"No luck?"

"The Clancys aren't interested in anything but full custody."

"But anyone could see Bonnie belongs with you," she said, gesturing to his hand holding the bottle.

"My lawyers think this is about anger. They're angry their daughter is gone. And they want the last link to her."

She nodded. "Bonnie."

"Yes," he said, gazing at his baby girl. "And they're angry at me because I have her."

"I'm sorry, Liam." Her voice was full of compassion, and just for a moment he let himself accept what she was offering. But only for a moment.

"Thank you, but don't be sorry for me—cheer me up instead." He grinned as he glanced up, wanting to just sit and listen to her speak in her beautiful accent. "Tell me about Larsland."

Her eyelids drifted closed as she rocked Meg. "It's beautiful," she said, her voice dreamy. "The sky is a blue I haven't seen since I left. The birds are different, so the birdsong early in the morning is distinctive. And the old cities on the main islands are a mixture of modern buildings and stone structures, some dating back hundreds of years."

As she continued to describe the sights, he glanced down at his daughter. Bonnie blinked at him as she drank, as if mesmerized. Her gave her a smile, then looked back to Jenna as she talked about her homeland, and suddenly he knew how Bonnie felt. Enthralled. He was enchanted by Jenna in the soft lamplight, by the glow of her skin and the emotion in her eyes. His body heated with heady warmth.

He'd never wanted to kiss a woman more.

Of course, the irony was that he'd never met a woman more off-limits. She was an employee, and he'd never cross that line and become a boss who made advances to women who worked for him. That type of behavior was deplorable.

Worse, Jenna Peters was the employee he particularly couldn't afford to scare off. Bonnie was the most important thing in the world to him, and Bonnie needed Jenna. If he made a pass at Jenna and she left, he'd never forgive himself. Being able to handle a night feeding on his own was a far cry from being able to look after his daughter's every need. Sure, he could get another nanny, but could he guarantee he'd be able to find one Bonnie liked as much? Whom he could trust as much?

No, kissing Jenna would be bad on so many levels. He held back a groan. Perhaps he should change the subject to something more practical, something she'd be less passionate about.

"I heard you met with Danielle again today." He'd asked his PA to meet with Jenna as soon as she could schedule it to get moving on the launch of the Midnight Lily and they'd now had two meetings in two days.

"She's great," Jenna said brightly. "We had our meeting while I changed diapers and carted babies around. She didn't flinch or lose her train of thought once."

Liam was pleased but not surprised. Hawke's Blooms was known for paying its staff well, but in return, they had high expectations of every employee. "Did you get far with the plans?"

"We made a list of what needs to be done in the next week, and she's going to liaise with people in Adam's and Dylan's offices. She's already booked The Gold Palm as the venue and they're talking about the guest list. I think everything's on track."

"Thank you again for agreeing to help with this. I appreciate it."

"You're welcome," she said, smiling. "It's actually been fun."

From the expression on her face, he didn't doubt that, but she was still doing him a favor. "I've been thinking, since you're handling this on top of your nanny duties, you should be compensated accordingly."

She held up a hand, her eyes suddenly serious. "I couldn't take more money. I'm barely doing anything—Danielle is doing most of the work."

"I'm not comfortable with you getting nothing. If you won't take extra money, then what?" He settled his gaze on her, wishing he could see inside her mind. "Tell me what you want, Jenna."

Jenna couldn't catch her breath. With his dark green eyes on her like that, her body quivered. What did she want? Him. No question. Just him.

But that wasn't what he meant. She bit down on her lip and looked away. "I can't think of anything."

He raised an eyebrow. "Then you're a rare person. Everyone wants something. What about a trip home to Larsland? We could wait until Bonnie's a bit older and get someone to fill in here for you for a couple of weeks."

Jenna stroked Meg's head as the baby's eyes grew heavy. "I'm not ready to go home just yet."

"Well, a trip somewhere else. Or if you don't want to travel, then perhaps a night out. Dylan's always getting tickets to Hollywood premieres and offering them to me. Fancy a night on the red carpet?"

An event swarming with media? She suppressed a shiver. The very last thing she needed was to be snapped in the background of a celebrity shot by a paparazzo and have the photo beamed around the world.

"I'll just take Meg next door," she said, glad her daughter had fallen asleep. She needed a moment to think of something to distract Liam.

After laying her daughter in her crib and kissing the top of her head, she went back to Liam and Bonnie. "The only thing I can think of is a puppy. Bonnie could have her own dog to grow up with her, and the puppy would be another constant in her life."

The royal court had several dogs, and one of the happiest memories of her childhood was when her parents had let her have a puppy of her own. The only stipulation had been on the dog's size. Because it would be living in a palace, it needed to be small and easily controlled. Her little Sigrid had been white, fluffy and her best friend. One day she hoped to be settled enough to get a dog for Meg, but there was no reason Bonnie couldn't have a little puppy soon—they'd just need to carefully supervise their interactions while Bonnie was so small.

Liam's gaze told her he hadn't been fooled for a second. "I have no problem with Bonnie having a puppy, but that's not something for you."

"I'd love a dog," she said earnestly, "so having one for Bonnie would be like having one for me too."

The corners of his mouth twitched. "Still not good enough. It has to be something else."

She released a breath and put up her hands. "Liam, honestly, this job is like a godsend to me. I have a home for my daughter and can spend all day with her." She looked down at the precious baby cradled in his arm. "Bonnie is the icing on the cake. I truly love her, and so does Meg."

Liam lifted the empty bottle from Bonnie's lips. "You'll have to teach me to burp her now, but—" he looked up at her, eyebrows raised "—we haven't finished on this topic yet."

"Noted," she said, hoping she'd have worked out what to say by the time they got back to it. She took the bottle from him and set it on the table, then grabbed a little towel. "Here, put this over your shoulder, then lift her so it's in front of her mouth."

He lifted Bonnie very carefully and positioned her. "Okay, now what?"

"Tap her back lightly, so she can bring up any air bubbles that went down with the milk."

The towel wasn't sitting quite in the middle of his shoulder and her fingers itched to smooth it out, but she knew he wanted to do this completely on his own, so she left it.

After a few taps, Bonnie brought up a small amount of white liquid, which, unfortunately, landed squarely on Liam's shirt. Jenna smothered a laugh as she said, "Don't worry, it's happened to me more times than I can count."

He turned his head to try and see the damage. "We might have to work on your aim, Bonnie Hawke. Or more likely, on my towel placement skills."

Jenna chuckled. "Here, let me take Bonnie so you can get that shirt off."

"Thanks," he said, passing his daughter. "She's one wink away from sleep anyway."

Jenna took the baby, whose eyes were already closed, rocked her a few times to make sure, then laid her in the crib. "Good night, beautiful," she whispered.

When she turned around, she was confronted by Liam's bare chest. He was standing several feet away, but he was all she could see, and a tiny spark of electricity shot straight through her. He was balling the shirt in his hands and looking around the room, probably for the dirty clothes basket, which gave her precious moments to observe him unnoticed. She took advantage of them without thinking.

His chest was solid with faint lines of definition and a sprinkling of dark hair. Her fingers itched to test the strength of the muscles there, to feel the crispness of the hair. Then she realized he'd stilled. She raised her gaze to his face only to find he was watching her. Her stomach fluttered. He took an infinitesimal step forward, as he reached out to stroke the side of her face then cup her cheek. His gaze fell to her mouth, and the nerve endings in her lips sprang to life, tingling. Yearning.

This was wrong, she knew it was wrong, yet in this moment she couldn't bring herself to care. All that mattered was Liam, and he was close, so close that her heart battered against her ribs.

He lowered his head, ever so slowly, until his lips brushed hers. Delicious warmth spread through her body and she couldn't contain the moan that escaped her throat. When his mouth settled more firmly and his tongue touched hers, she knew she'd reached heaven.

She fell into the kiss—into Liam. His heat and scent. Sensation danced across every nerve in her body. She reached up, touching his bare chest with her fingertips, and she felt a shudder rip through him. The shirt he'd been holding fell to the floor as one of his hands snaked out to press her fingers more firmly against his skin, the other to wrap around behind her, hauling her against him.

This kiss was more than anything she'd ever experienced—more intense, more uncontrollable, more glorious. Just more. And she'd never get enough. Of the kiss. Of Liam. He sucked her bottom lip into his mouth and she would have melted into the floor if he hadn't been holding her up.

And then he wrenched away, breathing heavily but with his gaze still locked on her. The air was cold on her chest where he'd been pressed only seconds before. The sudden absence of a kiss that had felt like her whole world caused her head to spin, and to stop herself reaching for him again, she rubbed her fingertips over her still tingling lips.

His eyes tracked the action, then he speared his hands through his hair. "Jenna," he said, groaning and stepping further away. "We can't do that again."

"I know," she whispered, trying to remember the reasons why. The job. She couldn't jeopardize the job and Meg's home.

Furrows appeared across his forehead, as if he was trying to force his brain to work. "Kissing an employee," he paused, swallowed, "is a breach of Hawke's Blooms' sexual harassment policy." His voice was a monotone, as if he was merely reciting the policy, while his eyes were still on fire.

"I don't work for Hawke's Blooms," she pointed out, then winced. What was she doing arguing a point she agreed with? They *couldn't* do it again. Shouldn't have done it in the first place. It was madness.

"No, but the principle is the same." He rubbed a hand down his face. "You have a right to a workplace free of inappropriate advances."

The guilt on his face tore at her heart. "Liam, don't get me wrong, I don't think it should happen again either, but just to put your mind at ease…you didn't pressure me. It was mutual." She'd been dreaming of his kiss for too long to deny it.

"Mutual?" he asked, eyes pained. "I'm not sure if that makes it better or worse."

She sighed, knowing what he meant. Resisting him would be so much harder now she knew he was thinking the same forbidden thoughts. She circled her throat with both hands as she willed her brain to kick into action. "Thing is, I can't start something right now anyway. Not with my life in such disarray."

He frowned. "What's in disarray? You have a job and a home. You and Meg seem relatively settled."

The blood in her veins froze. Had she given herself away? She silently cursed. This was the problem with letting your guard down—once it was down, there was no self-protection. No filter to protect your secrets. Thankfully, Liam seemed curious but not suspicious.

"You're right," she said as breezily as she could manage. "We are. I meant that I'll be returning to Larsland at some point, so starting something with you or anyone—it couldn't go anywhere."

"Well, at least we're in agreement," he said, ruefully.

She bent to pick up his shirt, needing to escape before she changed her mind. "I need a shower. I'll take this down to Katherine—"

"No, I've got it," he said, his voice low. He reached for the shirt and for a long moment, they both held the fabric, connected through it. She could feel the air pulse with the heat between them.

Then she quickly dropped her end. And fled.

Seven

"Princess Jensine?" said the voice on the other end of the line.

Jenna settled back into the sofa and held her cell phone closer to her ear. "Hi, Kristen. Yes, it's me," she said in her native language. "Can you talk?"

"Hang on." There was a pause and a muffled noise. The time difference and Kristen's shift work always made these calls to her friend in the royal security patrol difficult to plan, but they were the only way her family knew she was all right.

"Okay, I'm back," Kristen said.

Jenna tucked her feet underneath her, looking forward to a conversation in her mother tongue. "How are you?"

"I'm fine, but never mind that. How are *you*?"

"I'm good. We're good. This new job has been great—it has everything I need." Although it also had something she didn't need—an inconvenient attraction to her boss. An image of Liam rose in her mind: the way he'd looked two nights ago after he'd kissed her, his breathing heavy, chest bare, eyes brimming with desire. Jenna's skin suddenly felt warm.

"I'm glad to hear it," her friend said. "Any news on when you'll be coming back?"

Jenna's stomach dipped. She'd have to go back, but her parents wouldn't necessarily be pleased by her return. They'd definitely be angrier than they were with her now when they found out she'd had a baby out of wedlock. She'd been brought up to remember one golden rule: duty before all else. Duty before fun, duty before friends, duty before personal dreams, duty before everything.

And after they'd recovered from their personal disappointment, the focus would shift to how to protect the monarchy. In days gone by, they would have put Meg up for adoption or quickly married Jenna off to a husband willing to overlook her indiscretion and fudged the dates on official documents. With the advent of the internet, it was much harder to hide indiscretions unless she went completely underground, as she'd done. And she'd never consent to giving up Meg.

She just needed to find a solution that suited everyone.

"Not yet," she said, wincing at how inadequate that sounded.

"Your mother is becoming more insistent in her questioning when I give her your updates."

Jenna's heart hurt. When she'd first left, she hadn't considered how many people would be affected by her plan. "I'm so sorry to have put you in this position, Kristen."

The other woman blew out a breath. "I don't regret helping you, but I can't hold your parents off forever. So far they've respected your request for privacy, but I think that won't last too much longer. I wouldn't be surprised if your father is already planning to have someone in the Patrol track you down."

"Oh." Seeing them again and telling them everything would be hard enough, but being confronted by surprise, when she didn't have her thoughts in order, would be so much worse.

"You'll have to reveal the secret sometime," Kristen said.

"I know." And, despite knowing how disappointed her parents would be in her, she still longed to hear her mother's voice, to see her father's face.

"What can I tell them this week?" Kristen asked, breaking into Jenna's thoughts.

"Tell them…" What exactly? She chewed on her lip. That she was scared she was falling for the wrong man? That she wished she was a normal woman who could simply fall in love and not have to consider her duty in every situation, even when she was AWOL? "Tell them I'm fine," she said wearily.

"You know they won't be satisfied with that."

"I'm sorry, but it's the best I can do." Without a doubt she was going to have to find a way to fix the situation she'd caused, and soon. "Kristen, I'm sorry again—"

"Don't worry about it. I can handle this. It's no worse than that day when we were eight and you pushed me into the mud. My mother was furious I'd ruined my dress before the party."

Jenna laughed at the memory. "I was such a brat, even if you had just called my ringlets stupid. But you never told anyone it was me."

"That's not my way," Kristen said in her trademark matter-of-fact tone.

A ball of emotion welled up in Jenna's throat. "I miss you."

"Then come home." Jenna sensed an exasperated smile in Kristen's voice.

"I will," she promised, hoping to heaven that was true. "I just don't know when."

Liam walked through the back door and paused. Jenna was on her cell phone talking in her native language. The accent was light and musical, and without realizing it at first, he was smiling. The language suited her. Made him want to hear her whisper those musical words near his ear, to kiss the mouth that sang its sentences, to run his fingers through her blond hair as she spoke. He adjusted his collar, which was suddenly too tight.

Jenna looked up and saw him, and her face fell in unmistakable guilt. He stilled. Why? She was using her own phone, and he didn't doubt Bonnie was sleeping or taken care of or she wouldn't be relaxed and chatting. What else could she feel guilty about?

Was it a boyfriend? He shook his head as he dismissed the idea. One thing he knew—Jenna Peters wasn't a woman who would kiss him if she was already involved with a man.

Jenna ended the call and smiled at him, but it was a thin mask. Perhaps it had been what she was discussing that made her feel guilty. Had she forgotten the conversation wasn't in English so he had no idea what she'd said?

"Liam," she said overly brightly. "I didn't expect you home in the middle of the day."

He watched her face for any telltale signs as he spoke. "I thought I'd take Bonnie for a walk in the baby carrier. Maybe keep her with me for a while."

"That's a great idea," she said and slipped her cell phone into her pocket.

"Were you talking to someone from home? Your family?" He knew he had no right to pry, but still, he couldn't resist prodding just a bit.

"Er, no." Her eyes slid to the left. "Well, yes—a friend from home."

He prowled a few steps closer. "Is your friend in America now? I don't mind if you have visitors here at the house."

"Um, no. She's still in Larsland." Her voice was even, but the pulse at the base of her throat was rapid, her pupils too large.

"Do your family ever come over?" he persisted. "You're more than welcome to offer them the spare room next to Katherine's."

"Thank you, I'll keep that in mind." But her expression said she wouldn't. "I'll just get the baby carrier and Bonnie," she said, edging out of the room.

Liam watched her go, his gut in knots. Obviously more was going on with Jenna's family and homeland than she was prepared to admit. It shouldn't feel like a slap in the face that she hadn't shared that with him— she was under no obligation to tell him her life story.

But it felt uneven somehow.

He'd trusted her by letting his guard down and being open with her on more than one occasion—about Rebecca, about his fears of being a father, even about work and the Midnight Lily, which was still a secret from most people. Yet Jenna hadn't let him in on pretty much any level in return. Meg was the only person in her life that she talked about. Why was that?

And why did it sting like hell?

He raked his hands through his hair, swore under his breath and followed her up to Bonnie's room. Maybe they'd both be better off if he stopped obsessing about his nanny and let her have her damn secrets.

From this moment on, Jenna Peters was an employee, no more.

Two days later, Liam pushed away from his desk and pocketed his cell. His parents were about to board a flight that would take them to Oslo—the first leg of their journey home. He'd managed to track them down a day ago in the Faroe Islands to tell them about their new grandchild and they'd immediately cancelled the rest of their trip and bought new plane tickets. They were thrilled with the news and his mother was already planning presents and a belated baby shower.

He walked out of his office building into the sun and through the garden beds, on his way up to the house. Jenna would want to know that his parents were planning to visit as soon as they'd landed and been home to drop their bags and freshen up. He could have rung up to the house, but he was happy for the excuse to see his daughter.

As he walked across the back patio and neared the door, he could hear Jenna's clear, sweet voice; she was singing in her own language. When he reached the doorway, he could see her in the living room, sitting on the floor in front of both babies, who were propped up on the sofa, so their faces were all at the same height. And she was singing something enchanting.

Jenna glanced up, paused in her song and smiled.

"Hello, Liam. There's a little girl over here who will be delighted to see you."

Unable to resist either his daughter or her nanny—despite his promise to himself only two days earlier—he ambled over to the little group, picked Bonnie up and sat on the sofa with her on his lap. He'd done so well for those two days, keeping things professional with Jenna—though part of him had suspected he was only fooling himself, and any semblance of control would snap with one little crook of her finger. Still, another part of him clung to the belief that he was one hundred percent in control.

Jenna followed his lead, sitting beside him on the couch with Meg in her lap.

"Well, we're lucky, aren't we, girls?" she said, her voice playful. "A visit from Bonnie's dad during the day."

"Don't let me interrupt what you were doing with them," he said, putting his fingers out for Bonnie to grab with her little fists. "I only dropped by to tell you that my parents will be coming by tomorrow to visit."

Her eyebrows lifted in surprise. "I thought they were in Europe."

"They have been. It's taken me a while to track them down because they've been moving around so much, but they're coming home early to meet their first grandchild." He'd told them he didn't mind if they wanted to finish their trip, but they wouldn't hear of it. They could visit Europe again, they said, but only see Bonnie at this age once.

"Oh, that's lovely." Jenna smiled broadly. "And you weren't interrupting—I was just singing them a lullaby from Larsland."

Something deep inside him wanted to hear her sing

again…whether he was happy about that or not. He'd been charmed by her Scandinavian accent from the start, but hearing her sing had now taken his fascination with her voice to another level.

"Don't mind me," he said as mildly as he could. "Feel free to do whatever you'd be doing with them if I weren't here."

"All right then." She looked from Bonnie to Meg. "Where were we?"

As Jenna crooned the lullaby again, the babies stilled, transfixed. And Liam was just as affected. She smiled softly as she sang, looking at each girl in turn. And when she finished, she kissed each baby on the cheek.

"That was beautiful," he said once he could get his voice to work again.

She turned her bright smile—as dazzling as spring's first blossom—to him. "They like to hear singing, especially if it's our voices. You should try it."

He shifted in his seat. Her expression was so earnest that he hated to disappoint. "I don't know any lullabies. Well, I know fragments, but I can't say I remember any the whole way through."

She tickled Meg's sides, eliciting a giggle. "I'd sing one with you," she said, "but I only know them in my own language and that might be a bit hard for you to sing along with."

He tried not to seem thrilled that he couldn't be expected to sing. "You just go ahead on your own, then, and I'll listen."

"Bonnie would adore hearing you sing her something." Jenna tucked some of her silky blond hair behind her ear. "What about a song instead? How about 'California Girls'? No, something simple to start with. Do you know 'Edelweiss'?"

He nodded, resigned. "My childhood was filled with my mother watching musicals, so I could probably manage that one."

"What do you say, girls?" Jenna asked, tickling a baby with each hand. "Shall we give it a go?"

Jenna's hand brushed his thigh and his heart skipped a beat, but no one else seemed to notice. Meg squealed her delight and Bonnie's little legs started pumping.

"I think that's a yes," Jenna said.

She began the song, and after a few words, Liam joined in, uncomfortable at first, but once they reached the chorus he became more confident with the melody. Jenna moved into a harmony and his eyes strayed from Bonnie to her nanny. He'd never sung in front of anyone before, let alone in a duet, but it felt natural and… strangely, good with Jenna.

Her face shone and her angelic voice wrapped around him, lulling him into a magical place where anything was possible. She smiled when their last note faded away, so obviously enjoying having sung together that he closed the few inches separating them and kissed her.

At first, she didn't kiss him back, but she didn't pull away either, just let herself be kissed, and he was more than happy to oblige. Her lips were sweet, sensual, but not enough. He'd never get enough

Meg squealed in glee and they both froze, then quickly broke apart.

As he tried to regain his mind, Jenna blinked, then a fleeting frown marred her forehead and she turned to Meg and Bonnie.

"Did you know he could sing like that?" she asked them in a breathless voice. "We'll have to encourage him to sing more often, won't we, girls?"

It took him a bewildered moment to realize she was

going to ignore the fact that they'd kissed. He should have been pleased that she wasn't making a big deal out of it, but, for some reason, he *wanted* her to make a big deal, to be more affected. As affected as he was.

He drew in a breath, trying to get some oxygen to his brain. "I'm not so sure—"

"Bonnie loved it," she said, smoothly cutting him off. "While I'm thinking of it, you should take some photos of Bonnie soon too. You take such gorgeous, professional shots and you should capture this age. She'll grow up quickly."

"What do you mean by professional shots?" he asked, trying to catch up on the conversation. "I can take some snapshots of her."

"If you use the camera you use in your work, you could get some lovely portraits. We could hang one or two on the wall in here." She swept an arm, taking in the pale walls of his living room.

He shook his head. As a diversionary topic that she'd pulled out of thin air, it wasn't bad, but he needed to set her straight. "I don't have any experience in photographing people, but feel free to call a professional out, and make sure you get some of Meg for yourself, too."

"Liam, those photos on the bedroom walls aren't just snapshots. The lighting, the angles you've chosen, the whole package—they're good. Really good. You might see yourself as a scientist, but you're more than that. You have a creative soul. And deep down, I bet you know that."

For long seconds, Liam couldn't talk. Could barely think. Jenna had seen him in a way no one else ever had. Perhaps she'd seen through his façades more than anyone. Being with Jenna while he was with his daughter and learning about fatherhood meant he'd let his guard down. Kissing her was dangerous. He should never have done it once, let alone twice.

If he let his guard down and fell in love with someone who saw the real Liam and she rejected him—*rejected the real him*, the man he hadn't shown another woman—that would be a thousand percent worse than anything he'd suffered in the past.

Which was the reason he'd always kept things superficial with women. And one more reason he needed to back away from his nanny. Quickly.

"About that kiss," he said, his voice heavy with the emotions pulling at him. "I'm sorry. I won't do it again."

The corners of her mouth twitched. "You said that last time."

"And I meant it last time. I'm sorry for both times."

She sighed. "So am I. We have good reasons not to do it again."

"Your life is in disarray." Though he still didn't know what that meant exactly. "How about we don't bother with the reasons, and we simply agree that it's not a path forward that either of us is interested in exploring."

"That might be best," she said softly.

The aching sadness in her voice tore at his heart. "Jenna, just because I don't think we should repeat the experience doesn't mean that wasn't an amazing kiss." He looked her directly in the eyes. "It was. Amazing."

"It was," she agreed, then wrenched her gaze away.

He stood, gave Bonnie a hug and laid her back in the position she'd been in on the sofa when he'd arrived. "I'd better get back to work." He slid his hands into his pockets. "I'll see you tonight."

Then he turned on his heel and strode from the house.

* * *

The next day Jenna was sitting cross-legged on the floor in her bedroom playing blocks with Meg when Liam appeared in the doorway.

"My parents are here early," he said with an apologetic glance. "I should have expected they wouldn't be able to wait and would come straight from the airport."

Jenna jumped up, her mind clicking into gear. "Bonnie's asleep, but she shouldn't be for too much longer. I can bring her down when she wakes up."

Liam nodded. "I thought she might be. They said not to wake her if she was sleeping, but they'd like to meet you."

"Oh, right." It was reasonable they'd want a chance to assess the person looking after their granddaughter. She'd met them in passing when she was Dylan's housekeeper, but she'd never had a conversation with either of them. And now a proper introduction to Mr. and Mrs. Hawke took on more meaning—after all, she'd never kissed Dylan....

Liam scooped Meg up and tickled her under the chin. "What do you say, Meg? Want to meet my mom and dad?"

Thrilled to be in Liam's arms, Meg squealed and babbled, probably telling him about her day. It made Jenna's heart ache that Meg would never know Alexander and would lose Liam from her life when they left his house.

"Are you ready?" he asked, turning to Jenna.

She looked down at what she was wearing—a long floral skirt and a red tank top. She wanted Mr. and Mrs. Hawke to think their granddaughter was in safe hands. Would these clothes make a good impression? She had splatters on her skirt from the finger painting she'd done with Meg earlier, and her top was covered with creases from where Bonnie had gripped it in her little fists, but she figured because she was trying to make an impression as a good nanny, the look was probably appropriate.

She smoothed the skirt and tucked her hair behind her ears. "Yes, I'm ready."

Picking up the baby monitor, she followed him down the stairs, blowing Meg a kiss as her daughter watched her over Liam's shoulder.

When they entered the living room, Liam's mother came over and grasped Jenna's hands. "It's so lovely to see you again, Jenna."

Pleasantly surprised at the familiar greeting, Jenna squeezed the older woman's hands. "You too, Mrs. Hawke."

"Please, call me Andrea." She swept her arm towards her husband. "And this is Gary."

"All right. Andrea. Gary." She nodded at each one as she said their names, relieved that they already seemed to approve of her as their granddaughter's nanny. "I'm sorry that Bonnie's still asleep, but I don't think it will be long before she wakes."

"That's okay," Andrea said. "We can wait. In the meantime, we can keep ourselves busy with this beautiful girl. You must be Meg." She put her hands out to the baby in Liam's arms, then hesitated. "Do you mind, Jenna?"

"No, please feel free to hold her. Meg loves new people."

Andrea took the baby from Liam, and Meg looked around with quick movements until she spied Jenna, then smiled. Jenna gave her a little wave. Satisfied, Meg turned back to the new person she'd found.

Liam dug his hands into his pockets. "Do you want to freshen up while you wait?"

"No, we won't be here long." Andrea sank down onto the sofa with Meg, playing a game on the baby's fingers. "We just wanted to meet Bonnie, then we'll get out of your hair."

Gary turned to Jenna, his hands in his pockets, mirroring his son. "You're from Scandinavia somewhere?"

"Larsland," she said, nodding.

Gary broke out in a smile. "Ah, Larsland. That was on our itinerary, but we missed out when we heard about Bonnie and cut our trip short."

Jenna thanked the stars that Larsland had been one of the countries they'd missed. If they'd made it and seen her photo somewhere, they might have recognized her today. "It's a shame you missed it," she said, "but Bonnie will be more than worth it. She's an adorable baby."

Gary's eyes softened. "I'm really looking forward to meeting her. Perhaps we'll make it to Larsland next time. We'd even booked a tour at the royal palace. Have you been there before?"

Jenna froze. "Um," she said and swallowed. "Yes. Most people in Larsland have been at least once." She hated lying, but both statements were technically true.

Soft crying sounds came through the baby monitor. "I'll go," Liam said.

Jenna would have welcomed the opportunity to escape from a conversation that was veering into dangerous territory, but Liam was already gone. Besides, it was probably important to Liam to be the one who introduced his daughter to his parents, and she wouldn't want to deprive him of that.

Once Liam left, his father wandered over to the huge sliding glass doors at the back that looked over the flower farm and let out a deep, contented sigh. "The stock is looking good," he said.

His wife rose, Meg on her hip, and joined him. "There's nothing quite like that view."

Jenna followed them and gazed out at row after row of bright flowers that she'd come to think of as her own personal garden. "I don't know how you ever left it. I love waking up and seeing the flowers from my window."

Meg reached for her and Jenna put her arms out so Meg could monkey-crawl from Liam's mom across to her. Andrea smiled softly as she watched the baby. "After years of having the responsibility of a farm, we'd been dreaming of an apartment with no garden maintenance. No lawn, even."

Gary chuckled. "That sounded like freedom to us."

"I can see that," Jenna said, thinking of the times she and her brothers and sisters had talked about the freedom of a different life. "Sometimes responsibilities can feel overwhelming."

"The grass is always greener," Gary said, heavy on the irony.

Jenna cocked her head to the side. "It's not working out that way?"

Andrea shrugged delicately. "Oh, we're more than happy. And the change has probably been good for us. But I have to admit that, at heart, we're farmers. We're happiest with the feel of the soil between our fingers."

Gary draped an arm around his wife's shoulders. "There's nothing like tending to a seedling that grows and flowers into something bursting with color."

Liam's parents glanced at each other, and a look of sweet nostalgia passed between them. Jenna swallowed the lump of emotion in her throat. They so clearly had a deep love for each other, and their love for their career was inspiring. Had she ever felt that way about stepping into royal duties? Had her parents? When she'd been growing up, she'd taken it all for granted, which seemed such a waste now. If she had her time over, she'd look for the aspects of her role to love, find the joy.

She glanced up as Liam came through the door with Bonnie cradled in his arms. The sight made her breath catch, as it always did. He was so tall and broad that the tiny baby appeared even smaller, even more delicate, and the care he took as he held his daughter made Jenna's heart swell. In a few long strides, Liam crossed the room and passed Bonnie to his mother, the pride in his features unmistakable.

"So precious," Andrea whispered in a voice clogged with tears as she took her granddaughter. His father swiped at his own eyes, then hugged Liam tightly.

Touched by the private moment, Jenna held Meg closer and slipped toward the archway that led to the kitchen. Liam tracked her movement with his eyes. "Where are you going?"

"I thought I'd give you some family time together," she admitted.

"Oh, don't leave," Andrea said. "You and Meg are a big part of our granddaughter's world."

"Yes, don't leave on our account," Gary said. "Unless you have something else to do, of course."

Jenna readjusted Meg on her hip, torn. As Dylan's housekeeper, she would have melted into the background long before now. The thing was, she was still an employee, not a friend or family member. Yet part of her—the part that missed her own family with such aching sadness—longed to stay with the Hawkes a little longer, even if only as an observer.

Giving in to that feeling for once, Jenna sat down on the end of the sofa.

Seemingly satisfied, Andrea went back to inspecting her granddaughter, kissing her cheeks, rubbing her little arms. "Such a tragedy about her mother," she said. "For herself and her family, but also for Bonnie."

"It was," Liam said, his voice tight. Jenna knew that he'd do anything to be able to give Bonnie her mother back.

Andrea smoothed the dark hair on Bonnie's head as she looked up at her son. "What about her other grandparents? Have they been to visit?"

Liam's gaze flicked to Jenna for a split second, then back to his parents. "It's complicated. They're getting ready to file for custody. My lawyers tell me it should be any day now."

"They're *what*?" his parents said in unison.

"Apparently, they've been collecting evidence to prove I'm an unfit parent." He held up a hand to forestall their outrage. "Don't worry—my lawyers are on it."

"I should hope so," his father said indignantly.

Meg squirmed in Jenna's lap, so she put her on the floor and the baby crawled straight to Liam. As if without thought, Liam hoisted her into the air while still talking to his parents, explaining his meeting at the hospital with Rebecca's parents. His mother watched the move, then her appraising gaze swung to Jenna before a ghost of a smile flittered across her face.

Her stomach clenching at what Liam's mother thought she'd seen, Jenna abruptly stood. "I'll just get a bottle ready for Bonnie."

Liam nodded. "I'll help you."

Andrea Hawke broke out in a proper smile and asked her husband to take Meg from her son. "Don't hurry back. We'll enjoy our time with Bonnie and watch Meg for you."

Jenna felt the heat rise up her neck to her cheeks. Now she wasn't just hiding who she was from the world, but also how she felt about her boss. As she made her way down the hall, she cursed the tangled web she'd woven.

Eight

When they reached the kitchen, Liam noticed Jenna's cheeks were pink. "Are you okay? You look flustered."

She touched the tip of her tongue to her top lip, obviously debating whether she'd share what was on her mind. Then she winced and said, "Your mother thinks there's something going on between us."

"Does she?" He frowned and glanced toward the doorway that led to the hall. "What makes you think that?"

Jenna shrugged one shoulder. "There's a look in her eyes."

Perhaps he should have been paying more attention to his mother rather than watching Jenna. He scrubbed a hand through his hair. "Well, I suppose she's right. There is something between us. It's just something we've agreed we won't explore."

Her gaze flicked to his as she moistened her lips with her tongue, and all the blood in his body headed south.

"Jenna," he said, aware it sounded more like a growl than a word. "Since we both agreed it's not what we want, it would help if you didn't look at me that way."

Her eyes widened and she spun away to open random cupboard doors. "Your parents seem to have hit it off with Bonnie," she said in a rush.

"Yeah." He smiled, thinking of his daughter out there with her grandparents. "They've been hinting about grandchildren for a while. Probably since they retired and sold me this house."

"You know," she said slowly, turning back to him, "I think they regret that."

"Retirement?" He rubbed a hand over his chin. That didn't seem right—they'd been looking forward to retirement and the things they'd be able to do.

"I'm not sure about retiring, but I think they regret moving away from the farm."

He thought back over all the family conversations about his parents stepping down from the business and moving to an apartment. "That doesn't make sense. They'd been looking forward to a life of no daily responsibilities. A nice apartment in L.A. where they could walk to places and let the farm go."

"Maybe it hasn't lived up to expectations?" She took one of Bonnie's bottles from the cupboard and went to the pantry for the formula. "I don't know. It might be worth talking to them about it."

He narrowed his gaze as he tried to ascertain what she was getting at. "You think I should sell them the house back? Leave here?"

"No, sorry, I didn't mean that," she said, frowning. "It's your home now. Besides, maybe I'm wrong. Or maybe there's some other solution."

He leaned back on the counter and crossed his arms.

Could his parents be having second thoughts? And if they were, why had it taken an outsider to pick up on it? Jenna had only just met them.

"I'll keep it in mind," he said, surveying his nanny. This woman was constantly surprising him. And he wasn't at all sure how he felt about that.

It was just after seven that evening when Liam arrived home. Jenna had bathed both babies and gotten them ready for bed, and Katherine had helped her carry them down to the living room so she could get Bonnie's bottle and let the girls say goodnight to Liam. To Jenna's surprise, Katherine had taken to helping out if Jenna was struggling, which often happened if one of the babies wanted some attention while the other was having her bath. Jenna generally tried to bathe Meg when Bonnie was napping, but it didn't always work out.

"I'm sorry I'm late," Liam said as he came through the back door.

Jenna threw him a smile. "You don't answer to us, Liam. Besides, most nights you've been pretty close to the four o'clock finish time you said you'd aim for."

Katherine stood and hoisted Meg onto her hip. "Since we're doing apologies, I have one of my own."

The pronouncement seemed so out of character, Jenna was momentarily stunned.

"Katherine?" Liam said.

The housekeeper stood in front of them, expression as grim as ever, chin raised. "I haven't made anything for dinner tonight."

Jenna frowned. She'd ducked into the kitchen earlier to get a snack for Meg and seen a pot of pasta sauce bubbling away on the stove.

"But I saw—"

"As I said," Katherine said, cutting Jenna off, "I'm sorry. To make amends, I'll look after the babies, Mr. Hawke, while you take Ms. Peters out somewhere to eat. I'll keep Bonnie down in my room with me tonight and put the baby monitor in Meg's room, so don't you two be worried about how late you stay out."

Liam rubbed a hand over his chin. "I'm sure we'll make do. You don't have to—"

Katherine's spine stiffened and she fixed Liam with a glare. "Ms. Peters has been working herself ragged, between night feedings, painting the nursery and running around after these two. It's about time she had a night off and did something nice. We'll be fine here, won't we, girls?"

Jenna wouldn't have been more surprised if a bird had landed on the windowsill and given that same speech. Katherine had just come out on her side. Katherine, who seemingly still begrudged her presence in this house. Katherine, who'd not said a nice thing to her since she and Meg had arrived.

"Why are you looking at me like that? I have eyes. I've watched you work. Now, go," she said, making shooing gestures. "Go out for dinner somewhere nice."

Jenna still didn't move. Was Katherine trying to set this up as a date?

Liam grinned indulgently, then turned to Jenna. "Katherine makes a good point. How about it? I'll have a quick shower and throw on some clothes."

Katherine nodded, satisfied. "While you do that, I'll make you a reservation at George's place."

Jenna knew her mouth was gaping but was helpless to do much about it. One minute she was getting babies ready for bed, and the next, people were making plans around her.

Liam turned to Jenna, his eyes dancing with amusement. "Wear something nice. Katherine's brother is the chef at the hottest restaurant in L.A."

"That's assuming he can find you a table," Katherine said, clearly not willing to appear too kind all at once.

Liam gave Bonnie a kiss and then left, taking the stairs two at a time, and Katherine picked up the phone, leaving Jenna standing as if in the middle of a whirlwind, unsure of how her night had so drastically changed.

She was going out to dinner with Liam.

To the hottest restaurant in L.A.

Most worryingly, even though Katherine had planned it, why did that sound like a date?

Liam sipped his wine and looked around the restaurant, with its trademark high ceilings and pink marble and chrome interior, bustling with waiters and patrons. Katherine must have twisted her brother's arm to get this table—Liam knew they were normally booked out months in advance. And with good reason. His meal had been delicious, and if he wasn't used to Katherine's excellent cooking skills, he'd have been even more impressed.

A waiter cleared their plates and left the dessert menus.

"Would you like dessert?" he asked Jenna. Their conversation during dinner had been interesting. She was well informed on world affairs and they had discussed several scientific discoveries made in other countries.

Yet even while discussing topics as impersonal as science and world affairs, the insistent pull of attraction for her had lurked, and he'd had to be careful not to let his guard down and say something stupid. Something like, *Come back to my room tonight. I want to peel that pink silk blouse off you with my teeth.* His blood heated at the thought, and he tried to distract himself by studying the menu.

"I can never go past a cheese platter," Jenna said. "Would you like to share?"

"Sure." He indicated to the waiter that they were ready and placed their coffee and dessert order.

"You know," she said, looking around the restaurant with an expression of happy bewilderment, "I think this is the first night I've been out without Meg since she was born."

He cocked his head to the side, trying to imagine that. "Not once?"

She shrugged as if it were no big deal. Perhaps it wasn't to the many single mothers across the country. And probably half the married ones too.

"When I worked for Dylan, I took trips for groceries and errands while Meg was in day care, but nothing social. I never went out in the evening."

He didn't know how she did it. She seemed so calm and confident about being solely responsible for her daughter whereas he was filled with horror at all the perils that lay waiting for his baby girl out in the world.

He swirled the last of the wine in his glass as he asked a question that had been preying on his mind. "Do you think much about the future with Meg? About how you'll handle it on your own?"

She was silent for a moment before replying, and he became more aware of the background noise of glasses clinking and the dull murmur of a room full of people. Then she said, "Sometimes. Do you?"

He nodded. "And it scares the hell out of me."

The waiter returned with their cheese platter and

drinks. Jenna spooned sugar into her black coffee and stirred slowly as she regarded him. "I'm sure you'll find someone to share the parenting with, a stepmother for Bonnie."

She popped a piece of pear in her mouth and chewed. Liam put a finger in the restrictive collar of his shirt and tried to look anywhere but at her mouth.

"I'm not so sure," he said, wincing at both his reaction to her and his admission of the truth.

She threw him an ironic glance. "You're attractive and wealthy. Don't try to tell me you have trouble getting dates."

"Getting dates is one thing." He helped himself to a piece of blue cheese. "Finding a woman I'd be happy to have as Bonnie's mother is another thing entirely."

She trapped her bottom lip between her teeth and frowned. "She might not be the next person you date, but surely at some stage you'll find someone who would be a good fit."

"I tend to meet rich women, many of them professional socialites." He cut a piece of triple brie and put it on a cracker. "Or women who want to be," he said dryly.

"I hate to break it to you," she said, unable to hide her amusement, "but you're kinda rich too."

She was right. But he hadn't started that way. Maybe to Jenna, the difference wasn't obvious, but to him it was everything.

He took a sip of his coffee. "I grew up without much—some of the time my parents really struggled—and my brothers and I still have our working-class values. Any woman I'd consider as Bonnie's mother would have to have those same values, no question."

She arched an eyebrow. "There are a number of assumptions in your argument."

He knew that. He didn't doubt that it was possible for someone to grow up with wealth and privilege and still remain grounded, but he just hadn't met a woman like that yet. And if he hadn't met one so far, what were the chances of it happening in the near future, let alone that they'd hit it off and get married?

"Perhaps," he admitted, "but I'm sure you've seen the women Dylan dates. Glamorous and high profile. He attends red carpet events and knows who's who in the world of the rich and famous."

Jenna flinched. It was so quick that he would have missed it if he hadn't been watching her so intently. Then she composed her face into the dignified mask she usually wore for everyone except the babies.

"It's not a world you want to be a part of." It was a statement, not a question. She understood.

"I can think of nothing worse than attending events and having to smile and make small talk. Yet, like Dylan, that's how I meet women socially." He speared a piece of pear. "I think Bonnie and I will just have to make do on our own. And in the meantime, we have you, so all isn't lost."

"Yes," she said, her voice free of inflection. "All isn't lost."

But his gut felt hollow. Jenna was an employee; she wouldn't stay with them forever. He looked at her again and had an idea. Katherine had been with his family for years, and she seemed settled. Happy. What if he could make Jenna's working conditions so good, she stayed just as long? Starting with a raise. She'd certainly earned it.

The heaviness that had been sitting on his shoulders eased a fraction. Of course the flaw in the plan was that employees were off-limits, especially ones he was trying to retain in the long term. His plan presumed he could live with her down the hall for years and not kiss her again. Not touch her.

And he wasn't even sure he was going to make it through this dinner without doing that.

As they pulled up in Liam's Jeep in front of the house, Jenna tried to stave off her disappointment that the night was ending. It wasn't a real date. She couldn't let herself think that, and the sooner she was tucked up in her bed—alone—the better. Safe from fantasies that Liam had actually invited her out and that she was free to follow her attraction in whatever direction it led…

Then Liam leaned across and stroked her cheek with a feather-light caress, and all her attempts at being reasonable went up in smoke. She felt herself tremble under the touch but she didn't dare move, hope and doubts and anticipation warring inside her.

"Thank you for a lovely evening," he said and let his hand fall. That didn't seem to break the connection, though—it was as if the very air in the Jeep crackled.

There was no use denying she wanted him to kiss her, had never wanted anything more. And it didn't seem as if he was bothering with denial anymore either. His eyes darkened as he focused on her mouth. Her lips parted and she drew in a shaky breath, but he didn't come closer. The moment felt suspended in time, neither of them moving. Then his eyes changed, became pained, and his head swung away.

"We'd better go inside and check on the babies," he said and opened his door.

Suddenly cold, she blinked. The babies. Of course. She was the nanny, after all, not someone he was dating. But her traitorous body wasn't as easily convinced.

She pulled herself together and went with him into the house. Katherine had left a note on the hallstand saying that everything was fine, and Bonnie was sleeping soundly with her. They crept up to check on Meg, who was also fast asleep.

Jenna gave her daughter a soft kiss on her round head, then hesitated in the hall, unsure of how to end the night. There was so much unfinished between them that she had no idea of what to do, and Liam didn't seem to be in a rush.

Perhaps simplest was best. "Well, good night, then," she said.

"I always walk a date to her door." He waved an arm toward her room.

"Okay," she said, not really sure how to take that.

They took the few steps to reach her room, then she turned to look up at him. He propped a shoulder against the doorframe, his gaze smoldering. A wave of heat rushed over her skin, and suddenly she didn't want to do the safe thing anymore. Taking a risk was by far the more interesting option. She moistened her lips and hoped her voice sounded steady. "Isn't a kiss at the door part of that tradition?"

Liam stilled, studying her face. "You want me to kiss you, Jenna?" His voice was low and rough.

"Oh, yes," she said on a soft breath.

He groaned and his eyes closed for a heartbeat, and she thought she might never breathe again. Finally, his head came closer until his lips met hers in a kiss that was sweeter than any they'd shared before. Their other kisses had been stolen and had been all about attraction. This was more of an exploration, and more intense for it.

His hands found hers and their fingers entwined. When her knees wobbled, she leaned back against the door, and Liam pressed against her, not letting her fall. His body was scorching hot through her clothes and she wanted more, wanted everything.

Liam wrenched his head away, gulping for air, but his gaze didn't leave her. She'd never wanted anyone more in her life; her entire body vibrated with need. It was time for another risk.

"Can I invite you in for a coffee?" she asked as casually as she could manage, resting her hand on the doorknob.

His green eyes darkened, but the corners of his mouth twitched. "Thing is, because this is my house, I happen to know you don't have coffee-making facilities in that room."

"That's true, though I could probably rustle up a chocolate bar and a bottle of room-temperature water." She turned the knob and pushed the door open behind them.

"As it so happens, scrounged chocolate bars and room-temperature water are my favorite things in the world," he said, wrapping a piece of her blond hair around his finger. "But in all seriousness, Jenna, do you honestly want me to come in? Say the word and I'll see myself to my own room. It's your call."

She let out a long breath. "Liam, I can give you about five good reasons why we should say goodnight out here in the hall. And I suspect you have a list about the same length."

He raised a hopeful eyebrow. "But…?"

"I don't want to," she said simply. She'd been denying and fighting this attraction long enough.

His Adam's apple descended slowly, then came up again. "So what do we do?"

Good question. They couldn't go forward and they

couldn't not go forward. There had to be another way. "What if we give ourselves a free pass for tonight?"

Heat flared in his eyes. "The reasons we shouldn't do this aren't going anywhere," he said, tracing a fingertip down her throat. "We could park them in this hall and they'll be waiting here patiently to be picked up again in the morning."

"We wouldn't be doing anything wrong, because—"

He cut her words off with a kiss full of the passion they'd been holding back. She raised her hands to grip his shoulders, and his body shuddered.

"Because we're not brushing those reasons aside," he said against her mouth. "We're just—"

"Parking them for a few hours," she finished, her fingers tightening on his shoulders.

"Well, if we're parking them, it will be just as easy to park them in the hall in front of my room as yours. And my room has a bigger bed." He tugged on her hand and she followed him down the hall, anticipation bubbling in her belly.

When they reached his room, he drew her inside, then closed the door, pushed her back against it and kissed her again. "Maybe your room would have been better," he eventually said, leaning his forehead against hers. "That was a long wait between kisses."

With nimble fingers, he undid the buttons of her blouse. As he moved the fabric aside, his fingers skimmed and swirled from her stomach up over her bra, to reach the column of her throat. Her heart rate went soaring, her senses on overload.

"Jenna," he said, his voice uneven. "I've wanted you since the day you moved in."

"Only that long?" She gave him a crooked smile. "I feel as if I've wanted you forever."

He groaned and slipped his hands behind her to unhook her bra, then tossed it to the side. The air was cool on her breasts, but he soon cupped them, bringing all his warmth and the delicious friction from his work-roughened palms.

She slipped her hands under his shirt, feeling the play of muscles across his chest as he tensed in reaction to her touch. It wasn't enough. Trembling, she pushed the shirt from his shoulders and it dropped to the floor, then she leaned in and placed a kiss on his chest, thrilled when he sucked in a breath and held it. As her hands became bolder, roaming, exploring, he groaned and buried his fingers in her hair.

Part of her still couldn't believe she was here with Liam, the man she'd been watching, wanting for so long. But he whispered her name and she knew she wasn't dreaming. This was him, and it was even more perfect than she'd imagined.

He skimmed his hands up her thighs, bringing the skirt as he went, then hooked his fingers in the top of her panties and pulled down until she could step out of them, then out of her shoes. She was naked before him and he stared down at her with such longing that she felt as if she were floating.

He toed off his shoes, pushed his trousers and boxers off in one smooth motion, and then came back to her, kissing her until her head was spinning. She let her hands roam, wanting to touch him everywhere she could reach, from his biceps, up to his shoulders, and down the smooth skin of his back. While her hands explored, she kissed a trail down his body, loving that the muscles in his chest and abdomen tensed when her mouth made contact. And when she flicked her tongue out to taste the skin, he moaned her name.

He pulled her back up by the shoulders and held her in place with a kiss as his hands began their own journey, slowly moving down her sides, skimming the slope of her breasts, across her rounded stomach, and down farther. He broke off the kiss and dipped his head to take the peak of a breast into his mouth, just as his fingers found the apex of her thighs. She gasped, and he retreated, teasing, promising.

Just when she thought she could stand no more, he gently pressed her back on the bed and prowled over her, kissing and licking and nipping wherever he could reach. Then his mouth reached the core of her. At the first touch of his tongue, she moaned deep in her throat. His fingers joined the assault, and she could barely contain herself, as if she'd grown too big for her skin.

She clutched the sheets, helplessly giving herself over to sensation. Her hips flexed of their own accord, but his hands and mouth continued, slowly driving her out of her mind with the sweet torture, until all feeling coalesced and peaked at a point higher than she'd known existed and then shattered into a thousand shiny fragments.

She heard him opening a drawer in the nightstand. He retrieved a condom and quickly sheathed himself. But instead of coming straight back to her, he hovered, his weight resting on his hands on either side of her shoulders, his gaze locked on hers. The clarity of the look—no masks, nothing to hide behind—made something move inside her chest. It was if she was seeing into his soul. She reached up and ran her fingertips down his cheek, along his jaw, and when they reached his mouth, he tenderly kissed them.

Then he leaned down and captured her mouth in a kiss that was pure heat and desire and urgency. Without breaking the kiss, he positioned himself between her thighs, and she moaned deep in her throat. He entered her slowly, giving her time to adjust, but she wrapped her legs around his waist, urging him on, reveling in the warm rush of sensation as he began to move.

He rocked in a rhythm that she wanted to last forever and her body strained for his, wanting more, meeting every thrust of his hips.

She struggled for air, shifting restlessly on the sheets as the world pulsated around her. She gasped his name, over and over, could think of nothing else. Her body tightened around him. She was on the edge of something so intense, she wasn't sure she could handle it when it came, but if they stopped now she'd lose her mind.

And then he changed the angle and she fell over the edge of the world, falling, falling, soaring up, soaring as the world exploded around her, and she heard his words of release as he joined her.

Nine

Jenna woke slowly, surrounded by heat and male limbs. Still drowsy, and with the memories of their lovemaking lingering, she was perfectly content. More than that—in this glorious moment, blissful happiness filled every cell in her body.

She slid to the side, away from the weight of arms and legs, and propped her head on her hand so she could see Liam better. He mumbled something in his sleep and adjusted his body, and then his breathing became even again.

With his gorgeous face smoothed in sleep, he seemed relaxed as he never did when awake. But awake or asleep, there was no doubting his strong heart, his fascinating mind, his noble sense of honor. This was a man she could fall in love with…if she let herself.

A shiver ran across her skin. Of course, she would never let herself do that. It was time to sort out her life. She had to go home.

She had no idea how her family would react to her arrival, to Meg, but she had to at least tell them. Seeing Liam's parents with Bonnie had rammed that point home like nothing else could. Both her parents and Alexander's deserved to meet Meg. And Meg deserved to meet them.

Softly, she touched a fingertip to Liam's dark, wavy hair. She would give him notice so he could find another nanny, but she wouldn't deceive herself that he was merely her employer. Not while she lay naked in his bed.

She didn't know what they were to each other now, but one thing she knew without question—Liam deserved to know the truth. If she was prepared to share her body, then she should share the rest, too.

And she needed to tell him today. Before she gave notice, before anything else happened, she had to tell him who she really was.

She slipped out of the bed and found her clothes. After getting dressed and checking on Meg—and ducking into the nursery before remembering Bonnie was still with Katherine—Jenna grabbed her robe from her room and crept down to the conservatory to try to think of the right words. The words that would help Liam understand everything she had to tell him.

Unfortunately, she had to wonder if words that magical even existed.

Liam woke alone in the dark.

In general, that wasn't an unusual occurrence, but it wasn't one he expected to face tonight. Not after sharing his bed with Jenna.

Still drowsy, he'd reached out, hoping to find her ready to make love again, but instead he'd found the sheets cold. He'd grabbed his trousers and, zipping them up, headed for the hall.

His first thought had been that Bonnie had woken, but he'd checked the nursery, belatedly remembering she'd been with Katherine overnight. Then he'd checked Meg's room and Jenna's and, coming up empty, had started to worry.

He'd finally found her in the conservatory, sitting on the overstuffed green striped sofa, her arms wrapped around her knees in front of her. Her gaze settled on him, but she didn't move.

"Is anything wrong?" he asked warily, sending up a little prayer that she hadn't had second thoughts about sleeping with him.

"No." She chewed the inside of her cheek. "It depends. Maybe."

"Regrets?" he asked and held his breath.

Her eyebrows lifted. "About making love? No. I wanted you so badly I couldn't see straight."

He'd suspected as much but was glad to hear it confirmed. The feeling had been entirely mutual. "I like the sentiment, but I don't like how it was in the past tense."

"There's something..." she said with a slight tremor in her voice. "Something you don't know."

"Whatever it is, it can wait till morning. Come back to bed." He held out a hand and gave her a lazy smile. "I had plans for the rest of the night, involving you, me, my bed and none of these clothes we've accidentally acquired."

A smile flittered over her face, then was gone, leaving her features sober once more. "No, it really can't wait. In fact, I should have told you before I invited you into my room."

He wrapped his hands behind his neck and stretched.

"All right, shoot. But be warned, as soon as we're done here, we're going back to my bed." The heat began to spread through his body at the thought. "Those plans I have? They'll take the rest of the night."

She looked down at her interlaced fingers resting on her knees. "I need to tell you the truth. About me."

The truth about her? He stilled, suddenly focused. "Go on."

"Jenna is short for Jensine." She moistened her lips, swallowed. "My real name is Jensine Larson."

"You changed your name? Why?" That didn't seem so bad, if that's all there was, but seeing how serious she was, he stood a little straighter.

She looked up and met his gaze squarely. "I have a title that goes before my name. Princess. I'm from the royal family of Larsland."

Liam lost his breath for a full second. A princess? Here in his house. Less than an hour ago in his arms, welcoming him with her body. Of all the scenarios he might have expected, this had never rated a thought. A princess. Seriously?

He folded his arms over his chest. "I'm sorry, I haven't brushed up on my royal protocol lately. How close to the crown does one need to be, exactly, to be called a princess?"

She ran her fingers through her hair, pulling it back in a ponytail, then letting it go to fall over her shoulders again. "My mother is the queen, the current monarch. My father is the prince consort. My eldest brother is the crown prince."

Right. The daughter of the queen. It was so ludicrous he could have laughed. But he didn't. "And Meg?" he asked, though he had a feeling he already knew.

"If she had been born at home, and I had been married, she would be Princess Margarethe. Maybe she still is—I don't know how this will play out when I go home."

"Royalty," he said, still trying to get the concept to compute in his head.

She picked up her cell from the coffee table beside her and held it out to him. "Check online. I know you want to."

When he didn't reach to take the phone, she clicked a few buttons, then held it up for him. "That's me second from the left," she said as she passed him the device. This time he took it and gazed at the screen. "The photo is a couple of years old and my hair was longer, but it's still me with the rest of my family."

She had pulled up the official website of the Larsland royal family. "Princess Jensine Larson," he said slowly.

"Yes." Her eyes held a world of pain, and he didn't understand any of it.

He rubbed his eyes and sank down onto a sofa across from her. It really was true. His brain wasn't awake enough for this. "So what happened? How did you end up as Jenna Peters, nanny to Bonnie Hawke?"

"I was in love with a captain in the national army," she said, her voice so faint he had to strain to hear. "He was from an old family, and though we hadn't talked about it specifically, I think we both thought we'd get married one day."

His mind jumped ahead and suddenly he had a vision of Rebecca, pregnant with Bonnie, choosing not to tell him. His stomach hollowed. "Does he know about Meg?"

"He was killed in action before I could tell him I was pregnant." She seemed so small, so alone. He crossed to her sofa and wrapped an arm around her shoulders, but she didn't seem to notice.

"I'm sorry, Jenna." Such ineffectual words, but he could offer her nothing else. She'd said she was in love with Meg's father, which was so much worse than what had happened between Rebecca and him. He cast around for something to say. "I didn't know Larsland was at war."

She drew in an unsteady breath. "He was part of our contingent in a United Nations peacekeeping mission."

He nodded. Of course. This would have been a much smoother conversation if he had caffeine in his system. "So you were pregnant and single," he said, picking up the pertinent thread.

She shuddered. "Which is worse than it sounds. Larsland's royal family has prided itself for many years on the lack of scandal. You've probably seen that some of the other European royal houses have made headlines, so our parents instilled in us that it was our role to stay above that. Be better than that. We were never to give the people of Larsland a reason to question the need for a monarch."

Understandable but unnervingly hardhearted. "So they packed you off?"

She flinched, then tucked her hair behind her ears as if to cover for the reaction. "No, I left. I didn't want to put them in the position of having to make a decision about what to do with me."

"Hang on," he said, pulling away so he could see her face more clearly. "They don't know where you are?"

She winced. "Not exactly, no."

He thought of Bonnie disappearing when she reached her twenties and his blood turned to ice. He shifted away a little and rubbed a hand down his face, now really wishing they had waited till morning for this.

Then another thought struck. Without the use of diplomatic channels between the two countries, it would be beyond difficult for her to be here. "How have you pulled this off? Living here under another name is not an easy thing to achieve."

"I entered the country using my own passport, and since then, well, it's probably better that you don't know the details, so let's just say I have friends in high places."

He narrowed his eyes. "Friends who let a princess work as a housekeeper and a nanny?"

"It's what I wanted." She shrugged one shoulder. "I needed to be incognito for a time while I worked out what to do with my life."

Incognito. His chest clenched tight. She'd been using him. Toying with him and his family, starting with Dylan, then Bonnie and him. She'd lied, like every other woman he'd been involved with. The difference was, he'd trusted Jenna—she even knew how he felt about lying—but it turned out she was no different. His stomach turned.

"You've been using me, my family, as cover." Nothing since they'd met was what he'd thought. Their every interaction had been dishonest. She'd been playing him for a fool. "No one would suspect a nanny or a housekeeper," he said, disgusted.

She raised an eyebrow. "If you remember, you offered me this job. Pushed quite hard to get me to take it."

He shook his head, refusing to take that as an excuse. "You lied to me. I suspected you were hiding something, but I never imagined it would be on this scale."

"I know. I'm so sorry, but surely you can see why

I had to." She reached out a hand to him but he didn't take it, so she put it back in her lap.

"I can see why you had to lie to strangers, but to me? All this time, we've been living in a house together, and you've said nothing." He strode to the glass wall of the conservatory, acutely aware of how vulnerable they were in here—it seemed no better than being out in the open. "Do you even realize the risk you put Bonnie in?"

"No one knew I was here," she said, frowning.

"What if someone had found out? All it would take is one person who alerts the world's media that a princess was hiding out in L.A. as a nanny. If the media had descended on my house, we would have had no warning to prepare, to have enough security in place." The scene was almost too horrifying to contemplate. "You could have put Bonnie in the middle of a media frenzy."

Her face paled. "I honestly didn't think—don't think—that's a feasible risk."

"But it's possible," he persisted.

Her shoulders slumped slightly. "I guess so."

Liam felt so tense his muscles were vibrating. Tomorrow he'd meet with the head of security for the farm and work out an excuse to put in some extra safety measures. Even if Jenna left tonight, if the paparazzi ever figured out she'd once been here, this place would be crawling with the press. He'd never let Bonnie be a target.

"So what happens now?" he asked. "Do you want me to pretend to everyone that you're a regular citizen while you keep working for me?"

She unfolded herself from the sofa, wandered over to a stand of ferns and rubbed a frond between her fingers. "I need to go home and sort this out."

Something slid into place in his mind. "That's why you said your life was in disarray when we first kissed."

"Yes." She squeezed her eyes shut, and when she opened them again she seemed about ten years older. "I was always going to have to return home, and once I do that, I have no idea what the future will hold for me and Meg. It's not a time in my life when I can start a relationship."

"Right." He nodded once. The last thing he wanted was a relationship, either. Especially not with an incognito princess who'd been lying to him. "So you're leaving," he said, his voice flat.

"Not right away, unless you want me to." She raised her hand to circle her throat. "I thought I'd wait till after the Midnight Lily's launch, and I'll help you interview new nannies. Once everything's in place, I'll go."

He scrubbed his hands through his hair. "You know, this is not how I saw the rest of the night panning out."

"Liam," she said softly and waited till he looked at her. "I'm sorry."

"Tell that to Bonnie when she's crying for you after you leave." He knew that was an unfair thing to say, but he wasn't in the mood to be fair.

He pushed to his feet and headed back to his room.

Jenna didn't see Liam again until the next night at dinner. He arrived late, and she didn't blame him—if their positions were reversed, she'd have wanted time to process the bombshell she'd dropped last night, too.

"Good evening, Jenna," he said, his tone and expression excruciatingly polite. Which meant they were back to the mask he wore with other people but he'd stopped putting on for her. The realization stung but didn't surprise.

"Hello, Liam." She tried to be bright to compensate. "Bonnie's asleep, but she had a good day."

Katherine came in with bowls of steaming minestrone and freshly baked bread on a tray. Liam thanked her, Jenna said the smell coming from the bowls was divine and Katherine left with a satisfied smile.

Liam broke off a piece of bread. "I checked on her before coming in here and she's sleeping soundly. I had hoped to come in and get her and the carrier, but I was in meetings most of the day. Perhaps tomorrow you could ring Danielle when it's a good time for Bonnie, and I'll swing by and pick her up."

"That would be great. I know Bonnie would enjoy it." The mention of his PA reminded her of the meeting she'd had a few hours earlier. "Danielle came by this afternoon and we went over the plans for the Midnight Lily's launch. It seems to be coming together nicely."

"I've been thinking about that." He put his spoon down and met her eyes squarely. "The reason you don't want to attend is you're worried about being caught in a photo, isn't it?"

"Yes," she admitted, only just resisting the urge to fidget.

"What if we made it a masked event?" His voice was low, his gaze serious. "The Midnight Masque."

She gaped. "You can't make a change that big five days out from the event."

"It's not changing anything substantial," he said, shrugging one shoulder. "More like adding something. And sending the update to people who've already been invited will serve as a reminder about the event itself. I talked to Danielle about the feasibility earlier and she thinks it could work. In fact, she said there's a certain mystique to the flower already, so this will play up that element."

A masked event? She could see it in her mind's eye—guests wearing half-masks, the mystery, the glamour, the fun. They could bring their own or wear one that Hawke's Blooms provided in midnight blue. It could work, and she'd be able to see the fruits of her labor firsthand. It was perfect.

Without thinking, she reached out and laid a hand over his forearm. "You'd do that? After everything that I—"

He glanced down at her hand, his eyes pained, and she quickly withdrew it. Then he let out a sigh. "Regardless of what's occurred between us, this event wouldn't be happening without you. You deserve to be there," he said, his voice softening for the first time since he'd walked in the door.

A ball of emotion lodged in her throat, and she dabbed at her mouth with her napkin to give herself a moment. "I appreciate that. There's something I'd like to talk to you about too." If she were to leave, she wanted to ensure she left things the best that she could for Bonnie. "What do you know about Rebecca's parents?"

"From my own experience, they're rude and have a sense of entitlement. Although," he admitted, "they probably weren't at their best given their daughter had just died. From the private investigator's report, they seem like average people who have friends who think highly of them and others who are happy to speak badly. They've crossed people in business but also made allies. And the investigators couldn't find anything dirty going on in their company."

She wasn't surprised he'd had a private investigator look into them, or that they'd come out relatively clean.

She'd started to wonder if they were as bad as Rebecca had painted them. "What did Rebecca say about them?"

He buttered another chunk of bread. "She often made snarky comments about them, but the only specific thing I remember is that they're cold and manipulative. She said that when she was growing up, they were emotionally distant." He frowned. "Is there a reason you're suddenly so interested in the Clancys?"

"I've been wondering," Jenna said carefully, "if they were awful, why was she living with them?"

"That's a good question." He scraped a hand across the day's growth on his chin. "I guess I hadn't stopped to consider things from her point of view. In fact, she was apparently going to continue living with them when she left the hospital with Bonnie."

"And," she said, "more to the point, if they were such dreadful parents, why would she let them help raise her own daughter?"

Liam was struck by the comment. "You're right—that doesn't make sense."

"Did she have money of her own?" Jenna asked, gently probing.

"She did." He nodded, thinking back over Rebecca's situation. "And a part-time job in fashion. I assume she was on maternity leave, but she was hardly destitute. With her contacts, she should have been able to get another job easily when she was ready." Which meant there was no reason to believe she was with her parents for financial support.

"And she always had you as an option. Even if you parted on bad terms, surely coming to you for help with your own daughter was better than letting her cold, manipulative parents near her child, right?"

He wasn't comfortable speaking ill of the dead, but Rebecca had always had a touch of the drama queen about her. Exaggeration wouldn't be surprising. He'd assumed that part of her need for drama was because her parents had been the way they were, not the other way around.

He frowned. "Now that I think about it, it's possible, perhaps even likely, that she exaggerated their faults."

"And if she's exaggerated about them to you, can you imagine what she's said about you to them?"

He dropped his spoon to the table with a clatter as things finally made sense. "No wonder they're determined not to let me have Bonnie. Rebecca could have said anything."

He thought back over his first meeting with them in the hospital on the day of Rebecca's death. They'd been angry and scared for their daughter and had probably been told he was something of a monster, so when they saw him with their newborn granddaughter, of course they'd reacted strongly. In their shoes, he'd be suing for custody too.

Jenna tapped a finger to her lips, bringing his attention back from the past to the woman sitting in front of him. The woman he burned to touch again despite everything that had happened. He picked up his spoon and took a mouthful of Katherine's minestrone.

"You know," Jenna said, her voice puzzled, "I get that she might have talked badly about you to her parents, but not telling you she was pregnant is more serious. That's a passive-aggressive way of lashing out. Did your relationship end badly?"

Liam sighed. He'd been over and over this in his mind since he'd found out about Bonnie. "I didn't think so. I'd made it clear from the start that I don't do forever, that we'd never be serious. And she was okay with that. Said she preferred it that way."

"So why did you break up?" she asked gently.

"Nothing dramatic." He shrugged. "It just ran its natural course."

Jenna took a last mouthful of soup, then pushed her bowl to the center of the table. "Whose decision was it?"

"Mine." His chest hollowed out as he put two and two together. "I became uncomfortable when she wanted to spend her nights here. She started to push for more than I was willing to give."

Jenna laced her fingers on the table in front of her, brow furrowed in concentration. "Would she have known she was pregnant then?"

He shook his head. "I doubt it. I've counted back and it must have happened just on the cusp of us breaking up. She was getting clingy, but it wasn't because she was pregnant."

"Liam," she paused till he looked at her, "she fell in love with you."

"It's possible," he said, his gut churning.

"And you broke things off. Broke her heart." They were harsh words but not said unkindly. He knew Jenna was only trying to help, but it was still a brutal wake-up call. God, what had he done?

She'd loved him and he'd discarded her. He'd been a jerk. No, worse.

He groaned and sat back in his chair. "I never meant to hurt her."

She gave him a sympathetic glance. "I know. But when she found out she was pregnant, she couldn't bring herself to tell you. She punished you."

"I still deserved to know," he said fiercely.

She held up her hands, palms out. "No argument

from me. But we're discussing it now in a calm, rational manner. People make all sorts of bad decisions when they're emotional. Especially a woman who's pregnant with her first baby and panicking."

Something in her tone made him suddenly alert. "Are we talking about Rebecca or you?"

"Rebecca. Me." She rubbed her eyelids with her fingers. "I don't know."

Suddenly all the anger at her deception that had been bubbling away under the surface dissipated. This was harder for her than it was for him. "What are you going to do?"

She took in a shaky breath. "I shouldn't have waited this long to go home. Seeing your parents with Bonnie has made me think about my parents missing out on Meg. And Alexander's parents—they have a link to him that they don't even know about."

"The same link to Rebecca that her parents could have through Bonnie," he said, finally understanding where she was coming from.

Jenna gave him a crooked smile. "Why don't you hold out an olive branch to them? See if you can work out some arrangement?"

"They're suing for custody," he pointed out.

"If they thought they could be part of her life, and if they believed you were the best person to raise their granddaughter, perhaps they wouldn't feel the need to carry on with that case."

His father had often told him that if something sounded too good to be true, it usually was. It was a nice idea in theory, but reality was something else altogether. Too much water was under the bridge now. "I can't see it working."

"Isn't it at least worth a try?" Her voice was optimistic and damn difficult to resist.

He blew out a long breath. Anything was worth it for Bonnie. "You're probably right."

"You'll call them?" she asked, practically bouncing in her seat.

"I'll call them," he confirmed and just prayed this plan didn't make things any worse than they already were.

Ten

It had been six days since she'd told Liam her secret. Six days since they'd made love. Six days since her world had changed.

Each night after he arrived home from work, she'd coached Liam through another aspect of Bonnie's care, and last night he'd bathed his daughter. There wasn't much left for her to teach him, which was bittersweet. On one hand, everything was just as it should be; on the other, her presence was becoming less necessary by the day.

She'd made a deal with herself that if Liam's meeting this morning with Rebecca's parents went well, she'd be free to go home to Larsland.

There would be no more excuses left if Bonnie's entire family was intact and her father had all the skills to care for her. The last piece to fall into place would be to find another nanny, and if everything went smoothly with the Clancys, she'd talk to Liam about that today. She wanted this sorted out before the Midnight Lily launch event tomorrow night.

The doorbell rang and she heard Liam answer it—he'd asked Katherine to leave it for him. Jenna sat on the sofa in a long white summer dress holding Bonnie, who wore a bright pink dress and purple headband. Beside her was Meg in her best dress of tangerine and lime green checks, happily playing with her favorite plush dog toy.

Jenna's stomach was in knots. So much was riding on this visit—Bonnie's future relationship with her grandparents, the custody suit, the healing of a family. And the vow she'd made to herself about leaving...

She heard Liam's smooth, deep voice. "She's in through here, in the living room with her nanny, Jenna Peters."

Then Liam appeared through the archway, a tight smile on his face, followed by a middle-aged couple. The woman was carrying a teddy bear the size of a five-year-old child, and the man's face was obscured by a bunch of about twenty helium balloons in an assortment of pastel colors.

"Bonnie," the woman squealed as she rushed to the sofa. "Oh, my darling girl."

Jenna looked to Liam for guidance on how he wanted to handle Rebecca's mother, and in two strides he was beside her, lifting Bonnie from her lap.

"Would you like to hold her, Mrs. Clancy?" he asked.

"Desperately." She thrust the bear at Jenna with barely a glance and took Bonnie into her arms. Meg gurgled her pleasure over the teddy, and Jenna positioned it on the sofa so Meg could climb on it.

"Oh, my sweet, sweet girl," Mrs. Clancy said with

tears in her voice. "If the world was fair, your mother would be with you."

"I completely agree," Liam said, his tone and expression somber.

The woman jerked her head up, narrowed eyes fixed on Liam. "If only you'd shown that sort of consideration to my daughter when she was alive."

Liam bowed his head in a conciliatory gesture. "Mr. Clancy, Mrs. Clancy, I have to tell you I couldn't be more sorry with the way things have worked out."

Rebecca's father harrumphed. "You're only saying that because you want to convince us to drop the suit."

"I would like you to do that, yes, but it doesn't make what I'm saying any less true. I've recently realized," his gaze flicked to Jenna, "that Rebecca and I probably had different perceptions of what our relationship was."

Jenna's heart swelled to bursting. He'd taken their conversation seriously and was doing his best to make amends. He was a good man. An honorable man.

"You toyed with her," her mother spat at Liam. "It's what you do with women."

"Perhaps that's a fair comment, but Rebecca and I were always open about the limits of our relationship." He slid his hands into his pockets. "If I could go back and change things, I promise you, I would."

Mrs. Clancy looked pointedly down at the baby she held. "And Bonnie?"

"I love Bonnie with everything inside me. More than I thought it was possible to love." His eyes shone with genuine emotion. "She might have only been part of my life for a short time, but now she's my everything. My reason for getting up in the morning and my reason for coming home early in the afternoon. The center of my world and all my plans for the future."

Mr. Clancy scoffed. "I suppose this is what you're planning to tell the judge. Someone else probably even wrote those words for you to say." But Jenna could see they were softening, that Liam's heartfelt words had hit their target.

Bonnie grew restless and Mrs. Clancy tried to soothe her, but Bonnie had obviously reached her limit of time spent with an unfamiliar person and started to cry. Mrs. Clancy turned to hand her to Jenna, but Liam stepped forward.

"I'll take her."

The room stilled. Even Meg, always sensitive to the moods of the adults around her, stopped playing and looked around. The only sound was Bonnie's plaintive cries. The Clancys obviously hadn't been expecting Liam to back up his words with action.

Liam reached over and took Bonnie, putting her up on his shoulder so she was close to his face. Then he began to croon "Edelweiss" very softly. The love in his voice and in his every move was unmistakable and Jenna couldn't hold back the tear that had slipped down her cheek. Bonnie stopped crying and turned to see her father's face.

Jenna drew in a long breath. She couldn't deny it any longer. She loved him. Loved Liam Hawke with everything inside her.

She'd told herself not long ago that she wouldn't let herself fall in love with him, but that had been a staggering case of denial. How could she avoid it? The love was so big, so strong, she couldn't have outrun it. It simply was.

Not that he'd welcome her revelation. He'd been so exquisitely polite since the night they'd made love, she didn't know whether she'd killed any feelings he'd had for her, or if he'd smothered them in his anger. Either way, he'd made it quite clear that they had no future.

She gave herself a mental shake. The focus right now needed to be on helping Bonnie's family to come together.

Jenna looked at Rebecca's parents to see how they were reacting to Liam soothing Bonnie. Mrs. Clancy's jaw gaped, and her husband's aggressive stance eased before he dropped into a chair, the balloon strings still protruding from his fist. Meg clambered backward down from the sofa and over to Liam, trying to crawl up his leg. With his free hand, Liam reached down and scooped Meg up, and the babies' delight in seeing each other after an absence of minutes was clear in the noises they made.

Mr. Clancy cleared his throat. "Is there somewhere I can put these damn balloons?"

Katherine appeared in the archway, threw Jenna a wink and said, "I'm Mr. Hawke's housekeeper. I'll take them for you."

He handed them over without making eye contact. Seemed the Clancys weren't big on talking to underlings.

"Now, listen here, Hawke," Mr. Clancy said. "I'm not promising anything, but if, and I say if, we dropped the suit, we'd have conditions."

Liam didn't look up from the two babies in his arms. "Such as?"

"Regular visiting rights," Mrs. Clancy said.

"Input into decisions on her school," Mr. Clancy added.

Mrs. Clancy folded her arms across her chest. "You wouldn't move out of the area."

"A say in all important decisions in her life," Mr. Clancy said, pointing a finger to emphasize his demand.

Liam finally looked up, his gaze fixing on Mrs. Clancy before coming to rest on Mr. Clancy. "I will make all decisions about my daughter's future on my own. That's not negotiable. However, I'll take your opinions seriously, and I'll ensure you have access to her as often as is practical. A strong relationship with both sets of grandparents is a good thing for Bonnie."

Jenna watched the interaction with her heart breaking. Liam looked so strong, refusing to be bullied or swayed, yet fair and kind in his conditions. Oh, yes, there was no doubt she loved this man. He was going to make everything perfect for his daughter, and all Bonnie's family would be able to work together. This was exactly what Jenna had wanted for her little charge—a father with the skills to care for a baby and now a healthy, strong extended family.

But Jenna wouldn't be around to be part of it. She wasn't family.

She needed to go home, to see if she could salvage her own family bonds and give her parents a chance to know their granddaughter. She had no idea if that was even possible, but she had to try.

"Well," Mrs. Clancy sniffed, "I'll concede that it appears Bonnie is happy here. We'll consider the situation and let you know our decision."

"I appreciate that." Liam nodded once, confident, considerate. "Would you like some time with her now?"

Mrs. Clancy nodded but didn't rush to take her granddaughter, probably remembering that Bonnie had grown restless with her only minutes before. Catching Liam's eye, Jenna retrieved a play mat from the corner of the room and spread it on the floor, then relieved Liam of Meg.

He laid Bonnie in the middle of the mat, then turned to Mrs. Clancy. "Bonnie likes it when you play with the hanging toys. Especially the ladybug."

For half an hour the Clancys played on the floor with their granddaughter—occasionally whispering to each other—until Bonnie was ready for a nap. Jenna had already made her bottle and settled in on the sofa to feed her.

As they left, Mr. Clancy shook Liam's hand. "We're prepared to drop the custody suit, Hawke. But we expect you to follow through on your promise of regular access."

"You have my word," Liam said. "We'll stay in touch."

Once they were gone, Jenna turned to Liam and smiled, hoping to hide any hint of the realization that she loved him. "That went better than I expected."

As he let out a long breath, Liam sank down on the sofa beside her and lifted Meg onto his lap. "Thanks to you."

She shook her head. "You did all of that. I think you blew their socks off with your relationship with Bonnie."

"I meant in making all of this possible. This visit would never have happened without you. You'll always have my gratitude for that." For the first time since she'd told him her true background, he looked at her with something other than the polite mask he wore for most of the world.

In that precious moment, she glimpsed the real Liam again, saw his heart in his eyes, and knew he was as affected by her as he'd always been. So she had her answer—she hadn't killed whatever feelings he'd had for her. But then he severed the connection by glancing down at Meg. Clearly, he was unhappy about those feelings. Which was probably for the best. She needed to leave the States, and soon.

She pasted on a smile. "No need to thank me—I'm just glad that Bonnie will have as much of her family around her as possible. And now that that's resolved, we need to talk about hiring a new nanny."

His head jerked up. "You're really going?"

"I have to, Liam." Bonnie finished her bottle, so Jenna put her up to her shoulder, using the action to avoid eye contact with him as she said the hardest thing. "And to be honest, I don't think you're comfortable with me here anymore. Not after…" She trailed off, unable to say the actual words.

"No one could do a better job with Bonnie," he said, his voice rough.

She blinked back the emotion that threatened. "A good nanny will do fine, and you'll be more at ease without me here. I'll call an agency on Monday and set up some interviews."

Not replying, he took Meg over to the play mat and gently set her down. "Listen, I'll need to head into the hotel early tomorrow to help set up for the launch, and I'll take my clothes and get ready there. Will you be all right if Dylan takes you?"

Jenna said a little prayer of thanks that he'd changed the subject. She might have lost the fight against tears had they talked about her leaving for much longer. "Tell him not to worry. I can catch a cab."

"He's already offered." Liam shrugged and dug his hands deep into his pockets. "He'll pick you up at seven."

"Then thank you," she said. "That would be nice. The babysitter will arrive at six, so that will be good timing."

He started to leave, then turned back. "One other thing—I've arranged for a personal shopper to come out today with an assortment of dresses so you can choose one for the launch."

She frowned, unsure where that was coming from—the idea of him providing her with clothes made her think of mistresses. Did he feel guilty about sleeping with her? Or was it some misguided thought about her needing fancy clothes because she'd been brought up in a palace? "You don't need to buy me a dress, Liam." She had a perfectly serviceable black dress she'd been intending to wear.

"Jenna," he said, his gaze not wavering, "you're part of the organizing team, so your outfit is Hawke's Blooms' responsibility."

She narrowed her eyes. "You're buying a dress for Danielle and the others?"

"They'll all be wearing branded formal clothes, so people can seek them out and ask questions. So, yes, the company is clothing them for the night. And you as well."

Her lungs deflated. That made sense. And...part of her wanted to wear something other than the black dress. Wanted Liam to notice her again, no matter how unwise that was.

"Thank you," she said. "I appreciate it."

He gave her a tight smile. "I'll see you there."

Clinging to Dylan's arm, Jenna walked through the foyer of The Golden Palm, one of the most stylish hotels in L.A., and tried not to fidget with her masquerade mask. She hadn't seen Liam since he'd left after breakfast this morning, and all her deportment lessons couldn't save her, thanks to frustrating restlessness.

She'd chosen a silver dress with a fitted bodice and flowing skirt, but now she was wondering if it was the wrong choice. Perhaps she should have worn the satin yellow sheath with a split up the thigh that the personal shopper had recommended. The yellow dress had certainly been sexier—

"How are you doing, Princess?" Dylan whispered with a grin, interrupting her thoughts. Jenna had told him her secret on the ride over. Because he'd been kind to her as an employer, she wanted him to hear it from her. She trusted him, and she was going home soon.

She slapped his arm lightly. "It might be better if you don't use that word." She gestured to the throng of paparazzi clustered near the door up ahead, waiting for glimpses of celebrity guests.

He nodded his understanding and whispered, "I still can't believe my floors were cleaned by a royal princess. And that time I asked you to—"

"Dylan," she said firmly, "you gave me exactly what I needed at the time—a job and a home. You accepted me when I was pregnant, and you were a great boss. I honestly can't thank you enough."

Even though the photographers weren't interested in her, and she was wearing a mask that covered the top half of her face, she still looked down as they passed them and casually covered her mouth and chin with her hand.

"Tell me something," Dylan said as they entered the hotel foyer. "Is your new boss giving you what you need?" The mischief in his tone made the skin on the back of her neck prickle.

Unsure of where he was going with this, she chose

her words with care. "Liam's been good to me. And good to Meg. I can't complain."

"My mother thinks we might be welcoming you and Meg into the family soon. And just so you know," he said conspiratorially, "I couldn't be happier."

A wave of sadness, of powerful longing, washed over her. She knew Liam had no intention of proposing to her, and even if he had, she didn't have the freedom to simply accept. No matter how much she loved him, she had to do what she should have done from the beginning. Face the music.

She was going home as soon as she could find a new nanny for Bonnie, and as long as her parents didn't try to separate her from Meg, she'd consent to whatever plan they thought best for the good of the country, the monarchy and her family. This time she'd do what she'd been raised to do—put duty first.

But Dylan didn't know any of that. She hadn't told him her family was unaware of her location, just that she'd been incognito and that he needed to keep the secret.

She waved her wrist in a gesture she hoped seemed casual. "There's no chance of that happening, Dylan. I'll be returning to Larsland soon. But, for what it's worth," she said, smiling up at him, "you'll make a great brother-in-law to someone."

As they approached the doors to the ballroom, a woman in a midnight blue dress handed Dylan a Phantom of the Opera style half-mask.

"Thank you," Dylan said, slipping the elastic over his head. "How does it look?" he asked Jenna.

She grinned. "Stylish."

As they pushed through the double doors, Jenna couldn't hold back the gasp. The enormous room had been transformed into a night-time fairytale scene. A huge glowing moon hung in one corner, and shadowed clouds hovered in the air, suspended from the vast ceiling. Stars and constellations shone from above and from the walls, and occasionally a shooting star arced across the sky.

Tables set with crisp white tablecloths and covered in glassware, bordered the room. Huge stands of cascading flower arrangements, using a variety of white flowers, were artfully placed. Dylan and Jenna were a little early, so not many people had arrived yet, but a waiter glided over and offered them glasses of champagne. Dylan took one but Jenna shook her head. Her mother had never let them drink at official functions and the habit had stuck.

Dylan let out a low whistle. "Jenna, I think you may have just changed the way Hawke's Blooms announces a new flower forever."

"This wasn't all me," she protested. "Honestly, Danielle and the staff from your and Adam's offices have done all of this. This is so much more than I imagined."

"No," he said, holding up a hand. "You were the spark. It was one hell of an idea."

She gave him a gracious smile. "Thank you. I'm glad to have helped."

From the corner of her eye she spotted a familiar figure and, without thought, she turned. Liam was on the other side of the room, not yet wearing his mask; he was deep in conversation with Danielle, but his gaze was locked on Jenna. The sparkling room faded and it was as if he was standing within touching distance. Her skin warmed, and her pulse was erratic. Liam said something to Danielle, who nodded and left, and he began to cross the room to them.

"Oh, yeah, nothing going on between you two at all," said a voice beside her.

A dark frown crossed Liam's face and his gaze shifted to his brother, the warning clear.

"So," Dylan said when Liam reached them, "I was just leaving to investigate those ice sculptures. Lilies made of ice. Genius." Then he darted off before either of them could say anything. Not that Jenna would have been able to—she'd lost her voice around the time she'd spotted Liam in a tuxedo. Possibly lost her mind at the same time.

He cleared his throat. "You look sensational." He leaned in to kiss her cheek, lingering a little too long.

A ripple of heat ran across her skin, but she tried to ignore it. "Thank you for the dress. I love it."

"It looks great on you," he said, his eyes lingering as long as his kiss had. "Can I get you a glass of champagne? Or something else to drink?"

Her restless fingers needed something to do, so holding a drink was appealing, but she really shouldn't have one. Instead, she smoothed a hand over her French twist. "No, thank you. I'm fine."

His gaze followed her hands to her hair, then back to her eyes. "How were Bonnie and Meg when you left?"

"The babysitter had arrived and Katherine was in her element, explaining what she was required to do and showing her in no uncertain terms who was boss."

Liam chuckled. "We really should put on more household staff so Katherine can exercise her management skills." Then his face sobered. "I'm glad you came."

She felt a tremulous smile form on her lips. "I can't tell you how much I appreciate you making it a masquerade so I could be here.

Frowning in concentration, he picked up her hand

and held it between two of his. "Jenna, I know you're going home soon." He paused, cleared his throat. "I have the key to the hotel's penthouse room in my jacket pocket, and both the babysitter and Katherine are at the house all night with the babies."

Her breath was trapped in her lungs and she couldn't get her voice to work, but he didn't wait for her to reply.

"Stay with me tonight." His hands tightened around her fingers. "Being with you again…it's all I think about."

"Yes," she whispered before she'd thought it through.

His eyes flared, then he checked over his shoulder and winced. "I'm sorry, I have to help Danielle with some arrangements, but I'll be back."

Frozen to the spot, she watched him walk away. How would she ever make it through the night now she knew how it would end?

Eleven

Liam took a glass of white wine from a passing waiter as his eyes scanned the crowd for Jenna. The event had been in full swing for a couple of hours and he was only just getting a chance to catch his breath. Future events would likely be the responsibility of Dylan's or Adam's offices, but because the idea had come from his office this time and Danielle had been coordinating everything, he'd been the point man for the night. He wouldn't be sorry to lose the role—it had been hectic, especially when he'd only wanted to spend the time with Jenna.

Then he saw her, not too far away, chatting with his parents. Her silver dress shimmered; the fitted bodice drew his eye to her exposed collarbone, down over the slope of her breasts, to where the fabric tucked in at the waist then floated down to her ankles. His heart thumped erratically.

From the moment he'd seen her enter the room on

Dylan's arm, he'd been mesmerized. He'd never wanted a woman more. He was well aware that part of this need was a factor of the forbidden—not only was she his daughter's nanny, but also she was leaving. Tonight would be simple and pure, away from the complications of reality, as if away from time itself. Like Cinderella at the ball—except, of course, she was the princess and he was no prince.

A man walked into his field of vision, so Liam moved to the left and found Jenna again...and his movement made it obvious she was watching him from under her lashes. His entire body heated. Drawn as if by magnetic force, he found himself moving through the crowd until he reached her side. Their shoulders brushed and his heart all but stopped its beat.

"Liam," his mother said. "There you are. I was just telling *Jenna*," the subtle emphasis showed that she knew Jenna's real identity, "that if she needs to leave before you have a new nanny in place, I'd be happy to fill in."

Liam stiffened. She was thinking of leaving before they'd even employed a new nanny?

"There's no need," Jenna said quickly, her blue eyes shifting to him from behind the mask. "I have enough time to help Liam interview for the next nanny."

His mother nodded, smugly satisfied. "Have you noticed there's a dance floor over there? No one's using it yet. Perhaps you two should get it going."

He couldn't tear his gaze from Jenna and had only been half listening to his mother, but there was a pregnant pause in the conversation, he realized he must have missed something. "Sorry?"

His mother patted him arm. "Take Jenna over to the dance floor, Liam. Someone needs to start the dancing."

He grinned. That was a great idea. Danielle had been particular about having a dance floor, but no one was using it yet, so she'd appreciate him doing something about that. In fact, it was practically his responsibility as the point man to stand on that dance floor with this woman in his arms.

"Jenna," he said, holding out a hand, "would you like to dance?"

A slight blush tinged her cheeks as she laid her hand in his. "I'd love to."

Anticipation simmered in his veins as they threaded their way through the crowd to the two stairs leading to the raised parquetry platform set aside for dancing. He prayed the deejay didn't play a fast dance number first up. He wanted to be able to hold Jenna close.

The deejay saw them step onto the dance floor and changed the track to a Righteous Brothers ballad. Liam nodded his thanks.

As he put his arms around her, he sighed and pulled her close, and she wrapped her arms around his waist. She felt so good against him, as if she were made for exactly that spot.

He dropped his head to whisper in her ear. "I've barely been able to think of anything besides meeting you after this is all over. Tell me you haven't changed your mind."

"I have," she said and drew in an uneven breath. "About thirty times."

Another couple joined them on the dance floor, and, heart in his mouth, Liam navigated Jenna away from the interlopers so they couldn't be overheard. "And where do you stand right now?"

The tip of her tongue darted out to moisten her lips

and it almost undid him. "I…" she said, then swallowed. "I want to be with you one more time."

He closed his eyes and groaned. "I've been thinking the same thing." She would be gone soon, which was how it had to be—she didn't belong in his world and he didn't belong in hers—but in the meantime, they could make magic.

Two more couples began to dance, so she leaned up to whisper in his ear. "In fact, if you tried to lead me out of this room right now, I'd probably let you."

A shudder ripped through his body. "Don't tempt me. The official part of the evening is in half an hour and Danielle will murder me if I leave before then. She's putting me up on the stage."

"Half an hour isn't long," she said, tracing a finger down his lapel.

Not long? Incredulous, he looked down at her. "It's an eternity."

She smiled softly at him, her blue eyes dark. "You're right. It is."

More than forty minutes later, Jenna stood in the crowd as the well-known actor Danielle had arranged to appear cut the ribbon and a dark blue satin curtain fell, revealing the Midnight Lily. The audience cheered and clapped, but Jenna couldn't take her eyes off Liam, who was standing to the left of the group on the stage.

As the emcee explained how the flower was the work of Liam Hawke and his research team, Jenna finally turned to take in the audience's wonder and approval. She also admired the seamless presentation that Danielle had organized for the formal proceedings. But mostly, she was aware of Liam's gaze resting on her.

A message. A promise.

Her skin quivered deliciously.

After a witty final comment from the actor that sent the crowd into fits of laughter, the music began again, and Jenna's heart picked up speed. Liam would come for her now. She didn't take her eyes off him, willing him to walk faster.

As he threaded his way through the throng of people to her, he was waylaid every few steps by well-wishers. He spoke a little to each person, smiled, nodded and moved on, all while keeping her within sight.

Her hands trembled as she watched his approach and she put her water glass on a waiter's tray before she dropped it.

When he finally reached her side, he whispered in her ear, "Are you ready to go?"

The brush of his lips against her earlobe turned her insides to melted honey. "I was ready two hours ago," she said.

He took her hand and led her out into the foyer, then into the elevator. As soon as the doors swooshed closed, he put a hand at the nape of her neck and kissed her. She gave herself to the kiss, wanting nothing more than to be in his arms, to feel his lips against hers.

His breathing was heavy as he leaned his forehead against hers. "Jenna, I have no idea what I just said to those people. All I could think about was getting to you."

"I would have died if one more person stopped you."

The elevator doors glided open and he dropped his hand to her waist and inserted the keycard to the door of the penthouse suite in front of them.

When they entered the room, Liam didn't turn the lights on. There was no need. Every surface, from the coffee table to the side tables, was covered in flickering candles. Her heart tripped. The bed was a four-poster, with white diaphanous material draping the sides and tied back, and the white comforter was strewn with rose petals. A wave of goose bumps shimmered over her skin. It was even more magical than the ballroom.

Liam stood behind her with his arms wrapped around her waist and nuzzled the side of her neck. "What do you think?"

She slipped her mask off and let it drop from her fingers as she leaned her head back onto his shoulder. "When did you have time to arrange this?"

"I made the time." His hands strayed from her waist up to trace the slope of her breasts and the valley between. "Don't tell anyone, but this portion of the evening was my main priority."

She pressed back along his body and felt the thick ridge of his arousal against her lower back. He groaned in her ear, sending warmth blooming in the pit of her stomach.

"I've wanted you so badly all night," she said, turning in his arms so she could see his face. "No, before then. Since we last made love."

His breath rasped. "I haven't been thinking straight since that night. Tonight, seeing you in this dress, knowing you were coming up here with me after...it's been hard to focus on anything else."

She'd wondered if he'd been as affected as she, and it was a thrill to know he had. That this raging desire was mutual.

She pressed her lips to the skin on his throat. "I wanted you to kiss me when we were on the dance floor."

"I wanted to do this on the dance floor," he said, cupping her bottom and pulling her close. Being pressed against him so intimately sent a flutter low in her belly.

He kissed her gently, tenderly, and his chest rose and fell beneath her palms. His fingers burrowed through her hair, freeing it from the pins holding it in the French roll, and even her scalp tingled at his touch. Then he kissed her again, unleashing a hunger inside her that was fierce and demanding. She kissed all the way down his neck to nip at his collarbone, her eyes fluttering shut so she could focus on the feel of him below her lips, the taste of his skin.

Then she moved lower, opening the buttons of his shirt as she went, kissing the skin she exposed. His hands fell restlessly to his sides and then curled into fists, a shudder ripping through his body, as she reached his abdomen. When she undid the last button, she straightened and pushed the sides of his shirt over his shoulders. The candlelight threw a golden glow across his chest, accentuating the muscle definition, enticing her.

He reached for her but she stayed his hands. "Let me have a moment," she said.

Last time, he'd undressed quickly and she hadn't had a chance to enjoy the gradual reveal of his body. This time would be different.

She slid the button of his trousers through its hole and slowly lowered the zipper. His entire body tensed as she slipped her hand into his boxers and wrapped her fingers around him. This was one of the things she'd missed last time and had thought about since in the darkness of her own room. She glided her fingers along his length, luxuriating in the feel of him, glancing up as a breath hissed from between his teeth. The trousers lost traction and fell down his legs to pool at his feet, and she pushed the boxers down so he could step out of them.

Standing there, strong and glorious in his nakedness, giving her control of the situation, the power, simply because she'd asked, he was everything she could ever want. A ball of emotion lodged in her throat, but she swallowed it away—now was not the time. She lifted his hand and placed it on her shoulder and he took the cue, moving forward and kissing her softly. This was what she wanted—him. Just him.

He sank down to the edge of the oversized bed and pulled her to him until his cheek rested against her belly, and his thighs bracketed hers. She combed her fingers through his thick hair, losing herself in the sensation of his hands tracing her shape beneath the dress, over the curve of her hip, gathering the fabric, then dropping it again. The sweet torture was slowly driving her insane.

The warmth of his breath through the thin material sent shivers across the skin of her stomach. He turned her and unzipped her silver dress at the back, leaving it gaping. He turned her again until she faced him before he drew the straps from her arms and the gown slithered down her legs to land in a puddle. He kissed a trail across her stomach, the slide of his tongue sending electric heat rippling through her body, his evening beard rasping deliciously against the sensitive skin of her belly.

He hooked his fingers in the sides of her panties, dragging them down her legs, then turned her again to unhook her bra. When she faced him, he didn't touch, he merely looked, and the expression in his eyes—the hunger, the reverence—almost undid her. The peaks of her breasts tightened under his gaze, and shivers of anticipation rippled across her body. He cupped her breasts, brushing the tips with the pads of his thumbs, and her knees buckled. She was on sensory overload; it was too much.

"Liam," she said, knowing it was closer to a whimper than a word.

He tugged her off balance into his lap and she wrapped her arms around his neck, reveling in the hot, hard press of his erection against her thigh.

He brushed a strand of hair from her cheeks and whispered, "You feel so good in my arms."

"Well, your arms feel good around me."

He nudged her back onto the bed and stretched out beside her. Heat and anticipation rolled across her skin. She wanted him so badly—how would she live without him when she left? The thought was too awful, so she banished it as she scraped her nails across his skin, focusing only on Liam and the present moment.

He opened a bedside drawer and found a condom.

"That's convenient," she said, arching an eyebrow.

"When I ducked out to check on the room earlier, I dropped it off. I didn't want any obstacles for tonight."

She glanced around at the flickering candlelight. "You really did think of everything."

"As I mentioned, it was a priority," he said and rolled the condom on.

He aligned their bodies. His muscled thigh parted hers, and she trembled with the force of her need. She wrapped her legs around his waist, inviting him, and as he entered her, she moaned, dying at the pleasure but wanting more, always more. She wriggled, adjusting her position to take him fully, and then he slid further and the breath rushed from her lungs.

He began to move in a dance of advance and retreat, making her body sing. He moved faster, binding the coil of need inside her tighter, and she begged him to put her out of this sweet misery. His hand snaked down to where their bodies joined and suddenly she was tumbling, free-falling but completely safe because he would be there to catch her. He would always catch her. In that moment she knew that in her bones. And she would catch him.

Liam called her name as he found his own release, then slumped beside her and pulled her close against him.

Later, after she'd returned to Earth and Liam had fallen asleep, she realized she'd been wrong—they wouldn't always be there to catch each other.

She was going home.

And the longer she let it drag out, the more entangled they'd all become and the more she'd hurt everyone— Liam, Meg, Bonnie…herself.

A dark cloud seemed to engulf her as she thought about her future, but she had to be strong and make the right choice, not the easy choice.

Tomorrow she'd leave Liam's house for good.

When they reached home the next morning, Liam got changed and headed into work. It might have been a Sunday, but the launch had taken up a fair bit of time and his nursery team was behind on some orders, so he needed to spend a few hours in the greenhouse. And, hopefully, work out what he was going to do about Princess Jensine Larsen. Digging his fingers into soil always helped him think.

The first time they'd made love, he could excuse it as being impulsive. Giving in to temptation.

The second time? Not so much. They'd both had several hours to change their minds, hours to find an excuse, yet neither of them had. And he had to admit, he was glad. Their night together had been amazing, even better than their first time. And during the early hours of the morning, they'd made love again.

But…what happened now?

He lifted a tray of seedlings onto the wooden bench among the lush greenhouse plants and got to work.

He and Jenna couldn't go back to what they'd been before yesterday. Not after the intensity of their night together. But where were they headed? Where *could* they head? He might want her like crazy, but that wasn't enough.

A movement at the door had him looking up. Wearing a bright orange sundress, Jenna was walking past the African violets and orchids. She was more beautiful than the flowers she passed, but he noted a haunting sadness to her features. His belly dipped.

"Jenna," he said, "did you need me for something?"

She laced her hands together in front of her stomach and moistened her lips. "If you have a moment, there's something I need to tell you."

"Sure." He brushed his hands off on the towel beside him. "What is it?"

"I'm leaving," she said softly. "Today."

"What?" His head jerked up as ice hit his veins. "What about Bonnie?"

Pain and regret flashed across her features. "I'm sorry I won't be here to help you interview for a new nanny, but I've arranged with your mother that she'll look after Bonnie until you get someone. She's on her way over." A tremulous smile tried to form on her mouth. "She says she's looking forward to it."

Everything was moving too fast. "You promised you'd give notice."

She took a breath, her blue eyes meeting his squarely. "I'm asking you to waive that promise in these circumstances. I'm not leaving you without someone to look after Bonnie, and we both know this isn't a normal boss–employee situation."

Panic clawed inside his gut. She really was going today. "What if I asked you to stay? You've been happy here."

"I can't go on like this, Liam," she said, her voice breaking on his name. "It's tearing me apart."

"What if you stay but not as the nanny?" He cleared his throat, braced himself. "What if you stayed as my wife?"

A proposal hadn't been in his plans, but now that he'd been backed into a corner and made the offer, it felt right. She'd make a good mother for Bonnie and he'd have her in his bed every night. He should have thought of it sooner.

She raised her eyebrows, creating frown lines across her forehead. "And live the rest of my life incognito as Jenna Peters?"

"No." He straightened his spine. "Jenna Hawke."

"I can't live my entire life as a lie." Her hand fluttered up to circle her throat. "I'd be in hiding every day, wondering if anyone recognized me. And what about my family? They'd never know where I was. Besides," she said ruefully, "I think my father would have me tracked down eventually."

"I can't be part of your life if you go back," he warned. It was a deal-breaker for him.

"I know." She sighed, resigned. "You told me once that people born to wealth and privilege are a different species, one you have no time for."

"You can't believe that I think of you that way." Surely, after all they'd shared...

"No, but it's how you think of my family, of my real life. And I'm sorry you feel that way. You had bad luck and went to a rotten school when you were a kid, but I have friends and family who aren't like those people you experienced."

"I was raised with working-class values, and that's the way I want to bring up Bonnie." He'd put a lot of thought into this since he'd become a father, and his value system was the best thing he could pass to his daughter. He wouldn't compromise that, not for anyone.

"Not the way I was raised, you mean," she said pointedly.

He rested his hands low on his hips. "I won't commit Bonnie to a life in a royal family. It's the life you ran away from not so long ago. How could you expect me to allow that for my daughter?"

"So, we're at an impasse." She nodded, as if she'd expected this. "I can't stay, and when I get home, I'll be subject to my parents' decision about what to do with my life. And you won't be part of that."

A band clamped around his skull and tightened. He rubbed at the sides of his head—there had to be another way. His career was based on thinking outside the box and finding creative solutions. "What if they want you to stay out of the spotlight? To go on living incognito? You could come back."

"So, you'll have me under those circumstances?" Her blue eyes flashed. "You want to know something, Liam? I might have lied to you, but at least I saw you. What we had was more honest than anything I've had with anyone else, despite the lie."

He stilled as the truth of that statement flowed

through him. She was right. She'd been the first person outside his family to see the real him. And she might have even seen more of him than they had.

"I know," he said, his voice low. "I saw you too."

Her bottom lip trembled and she bit down on it before she replied. "You did, yes. But if I came back to a man who would only have me under certain conditions, what would that say about our relationship?" She swiped at a tear that made its way down her cheek. "It wouldn't be about the real me or you, the whole person. It would be about only accepting the parts that suited you. What sort of foundation for the future is that?"

He thrust both hands through his hair and held them there. What more did she want from him? He'd offered her marriage, then said she could come back if her parents didn't want her in Larsland, and still it wasn't enough. That was all he *could* do. Bonnie's welfare had to be paramount. What sort of father would he be if he sold out his daughter's future for his own happiness?

He set his jaw. "I can only offer you what I've already laid out."

"And I won't settle for less than what I need." She rubbed her eyes and turned to look up toward the house that was only just visible through the net walls of the greenhouse. "I've rung the friend who helped me move here, Kristen, and arranged to go home."

The weight of everything that had just happened suddenly fell down on him and he struggled not to let it press him into the ground. *She was going.* Jenna was leaving him and he couldn't stop her.

He covered the few feet between them and ran a hand down her arm to tangle her fingers with his own. "I'll miss you and Meg."

"We'll miss you and Bonnie," she said, her voice

wobbling. "If you need me, I've left Kristen's cell number on your bedside table. She'll be able to get me a message, no matter where I end up."

He leaned down to kiss her cheek, but, unable to stop himself, he drifted across and kissed her sweet lips instead. She moaned his name as she gripped his shoulders and he pulled her closer. She tasted of tears and everything he wanted, and he wondered if he'd have the strength to let her go or whether he'd hold her here in the greenhouse forever.

He wrenched his mouth away while he still could, stepped back and dug his hands into his pockets to keep himself in check. "Do you need any help packing?"

"No," she said, folding her arms tightly under her breasts. "I've packed a suitcase to take, and Katherine said she'd send the rest on for me."

"God, Katherine," he said, wincing. "She'll probably kill me. She's turned into your biggest fan."

She smiled, but it didn't reach her eyes. "I have to go. Your mother should be up at the house with the babies by now."

"I'll walk you up." He turned to his workbench and pushed the seedlings into the middle so they were safe while he was gone, then looked back to Jenna.

"Please don't," she said, gulping air as the tears flowed more freely down her face. "I don't think I could stand saying goodbye to you in front of other people."

He could barely speak past the lump lodged in his throat, but seeing her cry really tore him up. "Goodbye, Jenna."

"Goodbye, Liam," she said and rushed through the rows of flowers, away from him, gone.

Twelve

"Well, you're a sorry example of fatherhood."

On hearing his brother's voice, Liam scowled.

In the couple of weeks since Jenna had left, he felt like he'd merely been going through the motions of living, and Bonnie had been the only light in his dark. He hadn't felt like seeing anyone else and had barely spoken to the other researchers at work. So on a Sunday morning when he should have been surrounded only by his daughter's baby sounds, the last thing he wanted was visitors. Guests would expect him to talk and interact like a normal person, a person whose heart hadn't been torn in two, with one half on the living room floor here with him, and the other on the other side of the globe.

Resigned, he leaned over and picked up Bonnie from her play mat and faced them. "I'll be telling Katherine to check with me before letting you two in again. What's that comment supposed to mean, anyway?"

Adam shot Dylan a glance. "I see what you were talking about."

"What?" Liam demanded. He didn't have the patience for cryptic games.

Dylan winced. "Well, there's that bark for a start."

Adam reached over and took his niece. "A father should at least pretend to be enjoying time with his daughter."

Liam folded his arms over his chest. Who were they to question his parenting? "I was enjoying my time with her. Until you two showed up."

"Could have fooled us," Dylan said. "You look like you just lost the love of your life." His eyes widened in mock innocence. "Oh, wait…"

Liam felt his temper rising and cut his brother off before he could say something else and make it worse. "Why, exactly, are you here?"

"We wanted to see how you're doing," Adam said, concern in his voice this time. "Since Jenna left."

Dylan folded his arms, mirroring Liam's stance. "And if you're going after her."

Going after her? As if he hadn't thought about that option at least a million times. "I'm doing fine, thank you very much, and I'm not going anywhere."

Adam narrowed his eyes. "Then you're a fool."

"Hey!" Liam said, surprised. This was going beyond their normal fraternal teasing.

"You know," Dylan said conversationally, as if the other two weren't squaring off, "I was reading a Larsland newspaper this morning and I saw a story about our Princess Jensine."

Liam found his scowl again. Perhaps they'd been bored and were here to torture him for their own entertainment.

"They said," Dylan continued, "that she'd spent some time in seclusion after losing her boyfriend, Alexander."

"I'm not interested," Liam said, lying through his teeth. He'd wanted to check the newspapers too, but he hadn't allowed himself—it would be the start of a slippery slope that could easily end with him abandoning all his values and following Jenna to her homeland.

Dylan took Bonnie from Adam and spoke while he played with her fingers, as if this wasn't big news. "And it turns out that she has a baby, Princess Margarethe. The Larsland people have embraced them." He frowned. "I had to put it through a translation program, but I'm pretty sure that's what it said. Of course it could be they've got two new otters at the zoo called Jenna and Margarethe and the Larsland people have fed them. In some places it was hard to decipher."

Liam's chest expanded. Jenna had been worried about how it would all go down when she returned, but it seemed she'd been able to make peace with her family—at least enough that they'd presented her to the people again. She would be able to live the life she'd been brought up to live.

The life that was far away from his.

"That's good to hear," he said, ensuring his voice was even.

"Come off it, Liam," Adam said, throwing his hands up. "Don't try to deny you love her. We all saw it at the launch of the Midnight Lily."

Every muscle in his body clenched tight at being confronted with the truth in such a cavalier way. "Of course I love her. What's that got to do with it?"

"Are you intimidated because she's a princess?" Adam asked, rocking back on his heels.

Dylan nodded. "I can see why he would be. She was

too good for him before we found out she was a princess. Now she's totally out of his league."

"The door's that way," Liam said, planting his hands low on his hips and nodding to the front door. "Don't let me keep you from whatever it is you usually do on a Sunday morning."

"Yep," Dylan said, turning to Adam, "definitely grouchy. Seems we arrived just in time."

"She lied to me," Liam said before he could stop himself. "You can't build a future where there's no foundation of trust."

Adam sent him a mocking glance. "She had to. When she started here, she didn't know you from a bar of soap. Did you expect her to divulge a secret like that to a virtual stranger?"

"I saw you two together," Dylan added. "I don't care that she was lying about her name or her family. You two had something real going on."

"You know, I might have lied to you, but at least I saw you. What we had was more honest than anything I've had with anyone else, despite the lie."

Everything inside him seemed to tangle into knots. He used to think the relationships he'd had in the past were shallow yet honest. Both parties knew going in the game they were playing and the rules. But he'd been wrong. Very wrong.

He'd exposed his soul to Jenna, and he'd seen the essence of hers. Their time together had been nothing like the meaningless trysts he'd had in the past. Names didn't matter when the connection had been that deep.

But, he reminded himself, their connection wasn't the issue here. He straightened his spine and met his brothers' gazes squarely, one after the other. "Bonnie is my number-one priority."

Dylan looked down to the baby in his arms, then back to Liam. "Are you kidding? Bonnie adores Jenna and Meg. Letting her have them in her life *would* be prioritizing her."

"This situation is bigger than individual people. Anyone involved with Jenna would live their life in the public eye." He held back a shudder; he could think of nothing worse. "Remember the life Jenna has resumed is the one she ran from in the first place and ended up being your housekeeper. I categorically refuse to put Bonnie in that situation."

Dylan looked at Adam. "And you were right too. He *is* an idiot."

"Hey!" Liam said again.

"No family is perfect," Adam said on a sigh. "The best you can hope for is a family full of love. You love Jenna, and you love Meg. Bonnie loves Jenna, and Bonnie loves Meg. And Jenna and Meg love you both right back."

Had his figures-and-spreadsheets brother just used the phrase *family full of love*? At any other time, Liam would have laughed out loud.

Dylan nodded his agreement. "And you and Jenna are ridiculously well suited to each other. Any fool can see that."

"What more could you possibly be holding out for?" Adam said, exasperated.

Liam looked from one brother to the other, partly infuriated and partly touched that they cared enough to stage something of an intervention, and suddenly a thought hit him. The bonds with his brothers had been one of the most important things in his life, no question.

Bonnie had that with Meg. It was clear they had a bond—they already acted like sisters. And Bonnie responded to Jenna as a mother. She'd already lost one mother, so why was he letting her lose another one? Family was family.

Having Meg and Jenna in her life was more important than whether they might have to make a public appearance or deal with Jenna's family. Besides, Bonnie would have him on her side, which was one advantage that Jenna didn't have growing up. He'd protect her with a fierceness that anyone standing against her best interests would come to fear.

And if Bonnie would be happy because she'd have Jenna and Meg in her daily life, loving her, then the decision about their future rested solely on what *he* wanted.

He finally freed himself to admit it.

He loved Jenna.

Loved her and wanted her in his life, no matter that her royal lifestyle was the last thing he would have chosen. She was a package deal, and he was fine with that. More than fine. He'd put up with worse to have her in his life.

It was as if the world moved back onto its proper axis and clicked into place. This felt right. Felt good. Now that he knew what he wanted, he just needed to make it happen.

He lifted his daughter from Dylan's arms. "You two need to leave," he said.

Dylan was outraged. "I wasn't finished cuddling my niece yet."

"You want to stay," Liam said, throwing them both pointed looks, "then you can help. *Without* making comments. One of you can book me a ticket to Larsland. The other can find Katherine. I have arrangements to make."

His brothers slid each other a smug sideways glance, then jumped into action.

Liam watched them, trying to ignore that his heart was in his throat. Would Jenna still want him? Would her family approve of the match? Would he even get in to see her?

He took a steadying breath. He had more questions than answers, but he owed it to both Bonnie and himself to at least give it a try.

Holding his daughter against his chest and trying to keep his heart from beating through his ribs, Liam entered the palace's Throne Room. He refused to glance around, keeping his attention focused on the woman and man seated on the oversized chairs twenty feet away in front of a giant red velvet curtain with gold trim.

It wasn't hard to see the room had been built to impress and intimidate, with its two-story ceilings held up by huge columns, ornate moldings and decorations, and intricate murals.

The number Jenna had left in case he needed her had led to her friend Kristen, who, in turn, had started the ball rolling to get him here, meeting with the Queen of Larsland and the Prince Consort. After all the background checks and meetings he'd had with palace staff to get to this stage, Jenna's parents would be thoroughly briefed about him. If he wanted a future with Jenna and Meg, he needed to handle this royal thing head on.

And he did want a future with her, if she'd have him.

"Mr. Hawke," Jenna's mother said coolly. "So very lovely to meet you."

"Lovely to meet you as well, Your Highness," Liam said.

Jenna's father huffed out a breath. "We don't have

long. We've had to delay a meeting to give you these few minutes, so you might want to get to the point."

Liam held back a smile. No small talk. That suited him just fine. He adjusted Bonnie and faced them. "I spent some time with Princess Jensine and her daughter while they were in L.A."

The queen raised a regal eyebrow. "We know who you are, Mr. Hawke."

Right. Of course she did. But how much did they know? Just the facts from the background checks or had Jenna told them about him?

Had they told Jenna he was here…? His stomach looped. No, he had to focus on the present moment to be able to make it past this first hurdle.

He swallowed, then laid his cards on the table. "I'm here to request permission to ask Jenna for her hand in marriage."

Her majesty's face didn't move so much as an eyelash. "My husband and I are grateful for the assistance you and your brother gave to our daughter during her time in the United States. However we cannot give our consent."

The world fell away beneath his feet. He wouldn't let their refusal stop him from asking Jenna to be his wife, but he knew they'd just drastically reduced the chances that she'd accept him.

He straightened his spine. This wasn't over until Jenna told him it was.

Jenna stood with Meg on her hip, hidden by the thick velvet curtain behind her parents' chairs, trembling with the power of the emotions coursing through her.

Her mother had asked if she wanted to be present during this meeting, but Jenna had declined. Liam had contacted Kristen and asked to meet with the queen and prince, not with her. At first she'd been surprised, but she was also intrigued to find out what he wanted— she'd thought they'd said everything they had to say to each other before she left L.A.—so she'd accepted her father's suggestion to listen in instead.

When Liam requested permission to ask her to marry him, she gasped, then covered her mouth with her hand. Luckily, no one seemed to have heard, so she eventually let herself breathe again.

Those words had been the last thing she'd expected him to say. Was he serious? What could have possibly changed since she left?

Liam cleared his throat. "May I ask why I'm refused permission?"

"When Jenna returned," her father said, "she told us everything."

That was true. She'd resolved that going forward there would be no more secrets. She'd had enough to last her a lifetime.

On her first day in the country, Kristen had smuggled her in to meet her parents in private. She hadn't wanted anyone else to see her until her mother and father had decided what they wanted to do. She'd embarrassed them with a child out of wedlock, so it was their right to decide the next step.

The most likely outcome had been that they'd ask her to stay out of the spotlight—perhaps move to another country permanently—and come up with a cover story to explain her absence. Or perhaps they would let her raise Meg in the palace but tell the press she was someone else's child and that Jenna had adopted her. Or perhaps they'd come up with a plan she hadn't even considered.

But the parents she returned to were not the same parents she'd left. They'd been so frightened while she was gone, and blamed themselves for her disappearance, that many things had changed. They'd welcomed her with open arms and had been thrilled to find out about their first grandchild.

Then they'd called a family meeting with her siblings, the first one they'd ever had, and had an open discussion about what they all really wanted for their own lives. Not every wish could be accommodated, but the fact they'd been listened to meant her brothers and sister felt better about going ahead with devoting their lives to their country—something none of them questioned.

"And when she told us about you," her father continued, "we asked her if she'd like to marry this man from America, and she said no."

"She did?" Liam asked, his voice rough.

"She did," her mother confirmed. "And now that we have our daughter back, we'll be prioritizing her needs. So, no, you do not have our blessing."

Liam was quiet for a moment, as if absorbing that information. "You have to understand," he finally said, his voice like steel, "I won't give up. Not unless Jenna herself tells me she won't marry me."

Jenna's heart stopped beating. She couldn't wait another moment. She stepped out from behind the curtain. Meg squealed and reached for Liam, but she soothed her.

"Jenna," he said on a long breath. He didn't move toward her, which was just as well—she wouldn't have been able to think if he had.

She moistened her lips and found the courage to ask the question she needed to before they went any further. "Why do you suddenly want to marry me, Liam?"

"Jenna, you and Meg are half of my family," he said simply but with a world of emotion in his eyes. "I love you both, more than I thought was possible."

The air was suddenly too thick to draw into her lungs, but she persevered. Things were far from settled.

"My parents have offered me a full-time public role in Larsland." With them getting older and wanting to step back from some of the duties, and three of her brothers away in military training, they'd said at the family meeting they'd welcome the help. "How does that information affect your offer? A life lived in the public eye. Day after day, night after night, by my side, engaging in small talk."

She lifted her chin, challenging him, daring him. She needed to know if this was a misguided attempt to reclaim something that had been good while it lasted, or if he really could handle her life.

He swallowed, but he didn't waver. "Wherever you are, I'll be there. If you want to take on a job in Antarctica, Bonnie and I will join you. I realized after you left that family is family, regardless of whether the blood is red or blue. You and Meg are our family."

She took a step forward. "You would?"

"Without hesitation." He moved within touching distance and smoothly took Meg when the baby reached out and murmured a personal hello to her. With a baby in each arm, telling her she was his family, he'd never been more desirable. She'd never loved him more. "But I have a suggestion," he said and cast a glance at her parents.

Jenna waved away his concern. "You can speak freely in front of them. No more secrets. If we're to find a way forward, I want everything out in the open in my family from now on."

Liam shrugged a shoulder, then nodded. "In some ways, Bonnie and I will be grafted onto your family. In other ways, you and Meg will be grafted onto the Hawke family. You've already made changes to mine. My parents are meeting with an architect while I'm away to draw up plans for their new house on the farm's land. That's thanks to you."

"I'm so glad!" she said, thrilled that they'd be back where their hearts truly were.

"Sometimes," he continued, "families can be complicated, with their rules and expectations, as well as what we imagine the rules and expectations are. Especially when there are, ah…family businesses involved."

She couldn't contain a laugh. "I think both our families fall into that definition."

He tilted his head in acknowledgment. "So I have a proposition for you."

"I'm listening," she said and took Meg back when she kept thwacking Liam in the jaw. She needed to hear what he had to say before Meg did any damage.

"You and I can create a hybrid family." A hint of a smile turned the corners of his mouth up for the first time. "We negotiate with both our families. See how much my family needs me for Hawke's Blooms and how much they can do without me. I've already been handing over some of my role, also thanks to you. And we do the same with your family. We also do it with the Clancys, because Bonnie will still need access to her other grandparents. Then we look at what we want. You and me. And we create our family. One that suits us both."

For a moment she was speechless at the beauty of the plan. It was so obvious now that he laid it out, yet at the same time it was so quintessentially Liam with its hybrids and grafting. She tapped a finger against her lips and watched him watch the move.

Then she grinned. "You know, that could work."

She looked to her parents, who were listening to the conversation with indulgent smiles. They nodded their assent to his proposition.

Liam took her free hand with his and squeezed. "However we work it out," he said, low enough that she was the only one who could hear, "if you marry me, I'll spend the rest of my life making sure you don't regret it."

She felt the love she had for him rise up and fill her body, so much it overflowed and a tear, then two, slipped down her cheek. "You don't have to do anything to make sure of that," she whispered. "Just love me. Love us."

He cleared his throat twice before he could reply. "I can promise that, Jenna. I'll love you, Meg and Bonnie till my dying breath."

She'd forgotten the world around them existed, but suddenly her parents were beside them, and her mother kissed her cheek. "I'm happy for you," she murmured in their native language. "This is the right man for you and the right man to be Meg's father."

"Welcome to the family, son," her father said, patting Liam on the back, then taking Meg from Jenna. "This is a family that might take some getting used to, but Jenna will help you through it. And we'll be here if you need us."

Her mother put her arms out to Bonnie and Liam handed her over. "It seems we've acquired another granddaughter," she said to her husband.

The prince kissed his wife's hand. "It's been our lucky month."

Then her parents, holding one baby each, faded into the background, giving them some privacy.

Jenna reached up and cupped his cheek in her palm. "I can't believe you're here. I've dreamed of this so many times since I've been back that it still doesn't seem real."

His smile was slow and sexy, and it melted her insides. "Not only am I here, but I'm not going away. Not unless you come too."

Liam threaded his hands into her hair, then lowered his head and kissed her. The feel of his lips touching hers once more was sublime. She flexed her fingers into the front of his shirt and gave herself over to the kiss. Over to him. And when she felt the shudder that ran through him, she knew he was giving himself over to her too.

"From now on," he said against her mouth, "we're a team. You, me, Bonnie and Meg. A family."

Her heart swelled. "That sounds like a recipe for heaven."

Then she tipped her chin up and found his lips again.

* * * * *

*If you liked THE NANNY PROPOSITION, check out
these other sexy stories from Rachel Bailey!*

**CLAIMING HIS BOUGHT BRIDE
THE BLACKMAILED BRIDE'S SECRET CHILD
AT THE BILLIONAIRE'S BECK AND CALL?
MILLION-DOLLAR AMNESIA SCANDAL
RETURN OF THE SECRET HEIR
COUNTERING HIS CLAIM**

*All available now, from Harlequin Desire!
If you liked this* BILLIONAIRES & BABIES *novel,
watch for the next book in this
#1 bestselling Desire series,
SINGLE MAN MEETS SINGLE MOM
by Jules Bennett, available September 2014.*

COMING NEXT MONTH FROM

HARLEQUIN
Desire

Available September 2, 2014

HDCNM0814

REQUEST YOUR FREE BOOKS!
2 FREE NOVELS PLUS 2 FREE GIFTS!

HARLEQUIN

Desire

ALWAYS POWERFUL, PASSIONATE AND PROVOCATIVE

YES! Please send me 2 FREE Harlequin Desire® novels and my 2 FREE gifts (gifts are worth about $10). After receiving them, if I don't wish to receive any more books, I can return the shipping statement marked "cancel." If I don't cancel, I will receive 6 brand-new novels every month and be billed just $4.55 per book in the U.S. or $4.99 per book in Canada. That's a savings of at least 13% off the cover price! It's quite a bargain! Shipping and handling is just 50¢ per book in the U.S. and 75¢ per book in Canada.* I understand that accepting the 2 free books and gifts places me under no obligation to buy anything. I can always return a shipment and cancel at any time. Even if I never buy another book, the two free books and gifts are mine to keep forever.

225/326 HDN F4ZC

Name	(PLEASE PRINT)	
Address		Apt. #
City	State/Prov.	Zip/Postal Code

Signature (if under 18, a parent or guardian must sign)

Mail to the Harlequin® Reader Service:
IN U.S.A.: P.O. Box 1867, Buffalo, NY 14240-1867
IN CANADA: P.O. Box 609, Fort Erie, Ontario L2A 5X3

Want to try two free books from another line?
Call 1-800-873-8635 or visit www.ReaderService.com.

* Terms and prices subject to change without notice. Prices do not include applicable taxes. Sales tax applicable in N.Y. Canadian residents will be charged applicable taxes. Offer not valid in Quebec. This offer is limited to one order per household. Not valid for current subscribers to Harlequin Desire books. All orders subject to credit approval. Credit or debit balances in a customer's account(s) may be offset by any other outstanding balance owed by or to the customer. Please allow 4 to 6 weeks for delivery. Offer available while quantities last.

Your Privacy—The Harlequin® Reader Service is committed to protecting your privacy. Our Privacy Policy is available online at www.ReaderService.com or upon request from the Harlequin Reader Service.

We make a portion of our mailing list available to reputable third parties that offer products we believe may interest you. If you prefer that we not exchange your name with third parties, or if you wish to clarify or modify your communication preferences, please visit us at www.ReaderService.com/consumerschoice or write to us at Harlequin Reader Service Preference Service, P.O. Box 9062, Buffalo, NY 14269. Include your complete name and address.

HD13R

"**I** shudder to think how far you'd go to get what you wanted."

His expression tightened. "Yeah? Well, we both know how far you'll go, don't we?"

It was a cutting blow. When her father's will left control of Lassiter Media to Evan, it had resulted in an all-out battle between the two of them. Even now, when they both knew it had been a test of her loyalty, their spirits were battered and bruised, their relationship shattered beyond repair.

"I thought I was protecting my family," she defended.

At the time, she couldn't come up with any explanation except that her father had lost his mind, or that Evan had brazenly manipulated J.D. into leaving him control of Lassiter Media.

"You figured you were right and everyone else was wrong?" His steps toward her appeared automatic. "You slept in my arms, told me you loved me, and then accused me of defrauding you out of nearly a billion dollars."

All the pieces had added up in her mind, and they had been damning for Evan. "Seducing me would have been an essential part of your overall plan to steal Lassiter Media."

"Shows you how little you know about me."

"I guess it does."

Even though she was agreeing, the answer seemed to anger him.

"You *should* have known me. You should have trusted me. My nefarious plan was all inside your suspicious little head. I never made it, never mind executed it."

"I had no way of knowing that at the time."

"You could have trusted me. That's what wives do with their husbands."

"We never got married."

"Your decision, not mine."

They stared at each other for a long moment.

"What do you want me to do?" she finally asked, then quickly added, "About Kayla and Matt's wedding?"

"Don't worry. I know you'd never ask what I wanted you to do about us."

His words brought a pain to Angelica's stomach. He was up there on his pedestal of self-righteous anger, and she was down here…missing him.

Don't miss
REUNITED WITH THE LASSITER BRIDE
by Barbara Dunlop.

Available September 2014 wherever
Harlequin® Desire books and ebooks are sold.